Your Life, but BEtter!

Your Life, but BETTER!

A novel by
CRYSTAL VELASQUEZ

Delacorte Press

Copyright © 2010 by Crystal Velasquez

All rights reserved. Published in the United States by Delacorte Press, an imprint of Random House Children's Books, a division of Random House, Inc., New York.

Delacorte Press is a registered trademark and the colophon is a trademark of Random House, Inc.

Visit us on the Web! www.randomhouse.com/kids

Educators and librarians, for a variety of teaching tools, visit us at www.randomhouse.com/teachers

Library of Congress Cataloging-in-Publication Data
Velasquez, Crystal.
Your life, but better / Crystal Velasquez. — 1st trade pbk. ed.
p. cm.
Summary: As a twelve-year-old girl whose boring day at the mall turns exciting, the reader determines the outcome of the story by taking personality quizzes interspersed throughout the text.
ISBN 978-0-375-85084-4 (trade) — ISBN 978-0-375-89599-9 (e-book)
1. Plot-your-own stories. [1. Interpersonal relations—Fiction.
2. Friendship—Fiction. 3. Models (Persons)—Fiction.
4. Shopping malls—Fiction. 5. Personality tests. 6. Plot-your-own stories.]
I. Title.
PZ7.V4877Yo 2010
[Fic]—dc22
2009014433

The text of this book is set in 11-point Cochin.

Book design by Marci Senders

Printed in the United States of America

10 9 8 7 6 5 4 3 2 1

First Edition

To my aunt
Milca E. Pennulla
with all my love

Acknowledgments

First and foremost, I would like to thank my amazing editor, Stephanie Elliott, for giving me the opportunity to write this book and for being so creative and endlessly patient. Who knew our little writing group would lead to this? You're a pleasure to work with, and I'm proud to call you my friend. I can't thank you enough.

Thanks also to editorial assistant Krista Vitola, who provided valuable feedback on the first draft. Your suggestions helped turn a rough outline into a real book. Thank you!

Thank you to Jennifer Black, who did a wonderful copyediting job, catching all my silly mistakes. I owe you one! And thanks to Tamar Schwartz, managing editor; Marci Senders, designer; Natalia Dextre, production associate; Colleen Fellingham, associate copy chief; Barbara Perris, copy chief; Alodie Larson, proofreader; and the entire Delacorte Press team. I am deeply grateful for all your hard work.

I'd like to thank my whole family, especially my mom and dad, Madelin and Eliezer (a girl could not ask for more talented, caring, or amazing parents); my brother, Eli; and my grandparents, Guillermina and David White, for giving me so much love and support. You mean everything to me, and I hope I've done the Velasquez name proud. Thank you to my niece and nephew, Jasmine and Eli, for letting me borrow their names and for being so sweet, and to my cousins Melissa and David Viera, who competed for a mention in the book, making me feel like a real author. Congratulations!

You both win. Thank you to all my friends whose names I also borrowed. I'm so lucky to have friends like you. Your belief in me means a lot. And finally, to the readers. Thanks for picking up a book and proving that reading will never go out of style!

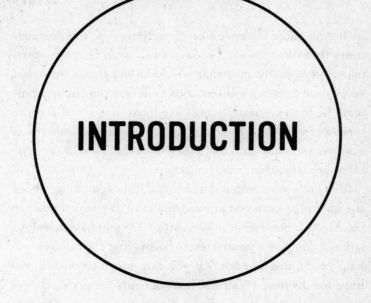

INTRODUCTION

Welcome to *Your Life, but Better*, the only interactive series that lets your true personality lead the way! You know what usually happens in these books: the reader gets to the end of a chapter, is faced with a random choice, and is told to decide what he or she wants to happen next. Well, not this time! This book is more like real life.

In this book, it's all about *you*! *You* are the main character, so the narrator always talks directly to you about everything that's happening. At the end of each chapter, you'll take a personality quiz that will help you figure out what you would do in a given situation. The outcome may not always be pretty, but it's honest. And just like in real life, the results of your decisions can be unpredictable. Some roads lead to love, fame, and fortune, while others lead to embarrassment, arguments, and rejection.

Along the way, you might learn a little something about the kind of person you are and the kind of girl you want to be. Are you book smart? Romantic? Do you have a jealous streak? Are you a good friend? Answering the quizzes will help you figure that out. All you can do is be yourself and hope for the best. (If all else fails, of course, you can always start over from the beginning and see where different choices might have led you. That part's a *little* better than real life.)

So go ahead; get started. What would you do on an ordinary day if something extraordinary happened to you? Start reading to find out. It's just like your life . . . but better.

Good luck!

chapter ONE

If the Ringling Bros. and Barnum & Bailey circus is the Greatest Show on Earth, and Disneyland is the happiest place on earth, then the downtown mall has to be the most boring place on earth. And yet here you are outside the mall . . . again. This must be your five thousandth trip here, and considering you're only twelve, that's saying a lot. You know the layout like the back of your hand. And if you have to look at one more scrunchie at Claire's Accessories or if one more cell-phone guy comes up to you trying to sell you a Sidekick, even though you clearly already have one on your hip, you're gonna scream! If not for the Pinkberry shop, a few cool clothing stores, and the occasional Jake Gyllenhaal movie showing at the Cineplex, you'd go stark raving mad. Usually your friends Lena and Jessie have to drag you here kicking and screaming. But today you have a feeling things just might be different.

"So you're sure Shawna's going to be here, right?" Lena asks, pulling her long brown hair back into a ponytail the way she does when she's getting ready to race someone on the track.

"Yes!" Jessie insists. "Her Facebook page was very clear. She said she'd be here at ten a.m. with twenty tickets to her ginormous thirteenth-birthday party. It's going to be amazing!"

You haven't had a chance to check out Shawna's page, but you know that when Jessie starts making up hybrid words—fantabulous, ginormous, wondertastic—whatever she's talking about is not just good, it's *gooooood*. But to you, this sounds a little too good to be true. "So what's the catch?"

"There's a catch?" Lena asks, stopping in her tracks. "Nobody said anything about a catch."

Jessie huffs and puts her hands on her narrow hips, the

stacks of silver bangles on her wrists jangling loudly. Now you've made her mad. She grabs one of your hands and one of Lena's and drags you both toward the mall. "Don't be such wimps. Of course there's a catch! I mean, sure, her family's doing all right, since her dad was smart enough to invest in solar panels. These days, you're nobody unless you've gone green, so all the celebs are buying those panels for their homes now. But she can't just *give* away tickets! The fact that her parents are splurging on this party is a big enough deal as it is, so she can only invite a certain number of people instead of the whole class. That's why we have just *got* to go. I doubt anyone else will even be having a birthday party this year, but Shawna's is going to make up for that big-time. Even Mona Winston is going. I hear she got Shawna to give her a ticket in advance somehow. I bet she'll be here today just to see who else scores a ticket."

"God, I hope not!" you exclaim. "That girl is toxic."

"No argument here," Lena adds, knowing how awful the new girl has been to you ever since she came to your school. "But anything that would even get Miss I'm So Much Better Than All of You to come here and mingle with the common folk must be worth checking out."

"Sounds like it has possibilities," you admit. "Even if it does mean wasting yet another day of our summer vacation at the mall. So what are the deets?"

Jessie takes an excited breath. "Well, the theme is going to be *Charlie and the Chocolate Factory*—the Johnny Depp version. Shawna is going to be hiding out in different spots in the mall, wearing disguises and stuff. If you find her, you have to answer a riddle or a trivia question or take a dare or something. If you get it right, you get a golden ticket to the party, just like in the movie."

"And the book," Lena is quick to point out without even looking up from her BlackBerry. The two of you share a love of books, which is one of the reasons you became friends in the first place. But Lena is one of those rare kids who prefer the book version of things to the movie version. She's never even seen the Harry Potter movies or *Twilight*. Freak!

"Right. *Fine*," Jessie says, rolling her eyes as she continues to tug on your arm. Any harder and your arm will come right out of your shoulder socket. "The book too."

"Thank you, kind madam. Now, please continue. What sayeth our good lady Shawna of what calamity will befall us should we fail in our endeavors?"

Jessie just knits her eyebrows at Lena. "Uh, would you mind saying that again—in English this time?"

Technically, it was English. Elizabethan English, that is. See, Lena is always falling in love with one author or another and then goes around sounding like his or her books for way too long. Right now she is in her Shakespeare phase, so she's been laying a lot of "forsooths" and "wherefores" on you and Jessie. (See above, re: Freak!) But Jessie can always count on you for a modern-day translation.

"She means what happens if we turn out to be the biggest losers in Loserville and get the question wrong?"

"Oh. That's easy. Get it wrong and you're stuck at home watching *Hannah Montana* reruns. Simple as that."

Lena shudders. "All right, all right, no need to threaten us!" You share a smile with Lena. You both know how much Jessie loves Miley Cyrus. Jessie has let go of your arm and has crossed her own arms over her chest. You're sure she's about to launch into Miley defense mode, so you squeeze your eyes shut and brace yourself for a recounting of all her greatest hits. Instead, you are greeted by silence. When you sneak one eye open to find out what happened to the verbal attack, you see Jessie smirking at you with a knowing look in her eyes.

"What?" you ask.

Jessie smiles and cocks her head to the side. "Why are you even pretending Shawna's party is the only reason you agreed to go to the mall today—as if you don't know that a certain comic-book geek could be walking those very halls?"

Doh! You were kind of hoping your friends had forgotten all about your little crush on Jimmy Morehouse, aka the most perfect guy ever. Well, maybe not perfect, but definitely way interesting. You've never had what could pass for a real conversation with him, but you've gathered all his important stats: he gets decent grades (he's no boy genius, but he does well enough to pass muster with Lena); he has no brothers or sisters; he's twelve years old; like you, he's kind of a klutz; and (this is the important part) he is the best artist you've ever met in real life. True, he mostly draws what Jessie calls boy stuff, like cars and comic-book characters, but whenever there's a school play, the drama club always gets him to paint all the scenery, and for months before showtime, he walks around with splotches of paint on his cheeks and T-shirts. (One of your "conversations" with him consisted of your walking by one of his freshly painted scenery boards for your school's production of *Grease* and mumbling, "Cool." By the time he turned around to say thanks, you had already scampered away so he wouldn't see you turn beet red.) And he never goes anywhere without his sketch pad, which in your mind just screams "Serious Artist." Any girl with half a brain would like Jimmy.

But why did your friends have to choose now to remember that you have half a brain?

"And there is the little matter of what you promised to do today if we managed to get an extra ticket," Lena reminds you.

You mash both hands onto your face, dread creeping over you. You know exactly what she's talking about, but in situations like this, which could cause death via extreme humiliation, you've always found it's better to deny, deny, deny. "I'm sorry; I have no idea what you're talking about."

Jessie lets out a simple "Ha!" meaning *Yeah, right.* You look over at Lena, hoping for a bit more sympathy, but she just shakes her head sadly while typing some code into her BlackBerry and then slips on the glasses she wears only for reading. "Tsk, tsk, tsk . . . I was afraid you'd say that. Good thing I have a written record of our oral agreement on my blog."

"Your blog?" you screech. "Please, *please* tell me you haven't posted anything on the Internet about me."

"Relax," Lena says calmly as she presses a few keys, seemingly scrolling through various blog entries. "I've changed all the names to protect the innocent. Besides, I haven't taken the blog public . . . yet. I just started it because having created one at my age is going to look awesome on my college applications one day. Ah yes, here we are. Last Saturday at exactly nine-oh-two p.m. during a sleepover at Jessie's house, you said, and I quote, 'Fine. The next time I see him, I'll ask him if he wants to hang out with me, all right? Now can you please pass the nachos already?'" Lena peers at you over the top of her glasses. "I have to tell you I didn't care for your tone. Such hostility!"

Your eyes bug out of your head. "Are you for real? You actually expect me to follow through with something I said while drinking way too much soda and playing Truth or Dare? Obviously I wasn't in my right mind. No way would that hold up in court."

"Uh, sorry, but I have to disagree with you there," Jessie interjects. "The rules of Truth or Dare are pretty much written in stone. I heard Britney Spears even got married once because somebody dared her to, so, you know, this is serious business."

Leave it to Jessie to cite Britney as a reliable source.

You sigh, feeling outnumbered. You're not even sure

Jimmy will be at the mall today and already you can feel your palms sweating. "Okay, okay, but what if I . . . I mean, what if he . . . ?" you stammer, picturing all the horrible possibilities.

Lena squeezes your shoulder reassuringly. "Hey, you've liked him for a long time, right?"

You shrug one shoulder while staring at your shoelaces.

"You think he's nice and you two might have some stuff in common, right?"

"I guess."

"So it wouldn't hurt to at least try to get to know him better as friends, right?"

"Dang it, Lena, can you please stop making so much sense?"

She smiles and puts her BlackBerry into her backpack, then slings the bag over her shoulder. "Now all you have to decide is where you want to ask him to go."

"Duuuh!" Jessie says loudly. "Isn't it obvious? If you win a ticket, you can ask him to go with you to the party. It would be perfect!"

"Would they really let you bring someone?" asks Lena.

"I'm not sure," Jessie answers quickly. "But there's only one way to find out. So if we can get past this very touching *Tyra Show* moment, can we please go inside now and get in the game?"

"I'm in!" Lena chimes, a competitive gleam in her eye.

And with that, the three of you file into the mall through the revolving door.

"Well, at least it looks like we're the only ones here so far, so we'll have Shawna and her golden tickets all to our . . ." You trail off as your eyes adjust to the fluorescent lights. Whoa! Half the kids from your grade are here, milling around the hallway.

You see Charlie Daniels sitting on a bench, studying a large color-coded map of the mall. Everybody knows that Charlie is a businessman in the making, so it doesn't surprise you at all that he took the time to download a map off the Internet and is now no doubt marking what he thinks will be the most efficient route. He's even wearing a tie. You've always thought he and Lena would be the perfect partners in crime. And something about the way Lena is nodding approvingly at his businesslike charts tells you she might think so too. But since flirting with boys isn't something she can add to her future college applications, it's not exactly high on her list.

Meanwhile, Lizette Tores and her two cousins, Delia and Celia, are looking through a rack of clothes in front of the Aéropostale store. Delia and Celia are arguing about a red pullover. You can hear them bickering from here. "I saw it first!" they're crying in unison.

"No, I did! Why do you always have to be such a copy-cat?" Poor Lizette just moves to another rack, trying her best to ignore the shouting, which seems to be in surround sound. Being a year older than the twins has made her their automatic babysitter, so wherever she goes, they're never far behind.

You glance over at Jessie and you can tell by her narrowed eyes that she's sizing up the rest of your competition. There's Mark Bukowski, surrounded by his baseball-team buddies, taking bets on who will find Shawna first.

There's Jasmine Viera, teacher's pet and all-around know-it-all. She could be big competition, because she's a well of useless information. But she just got her braces off a couple of days ago and is too busy staring at her own teeth in a compact mirror to focus on Shawna.

Eli Santini might be a bit more of a problem. He's way taller than the average sixth grader, so that could help him see over crowds of people, allowing him to spot the birthday girl before anybody else does. And everybody knows that Shawna has a crush on him. If he finds her, even if he gets his answer wrong, Shawna will probably give him a ticket anyway.

Then there are the Grain brothers, Nick and Andy. If you had to vote on which two kids in your school would be most likely to win on *Survivor*, you would pick those two. They're built like linebackers and willing to eat anything, no matter how gross it is, and as far as you know, they have never, ever turned down a dare.

"So much for us being the first ones here," you say with a sigh. But you still have faith in your three-person crew: Lena Saldano, track star extraordinaire, bookworm, and certified tomboy; Jessie Miller, goddess of all things popular and fashionista-in-training; and you, the glue that holds it all together. You're sure that between the three of you, you've got this thing in the bag.

Just then, Amy Choi, the biggest gossip in the school, comes running up to you and your friends. "Oh. My. God!" she cries. "You guys are here too! Today is going to be so crazy. I heard Shawna's been here for hours already and that she has secret cameras set up all over the mall!"

"That's not true . . . is it?" Lena asks, glancing around suspiciously. It's a well-known fact that you can believe only half of whatever Amy tells you. She doesn't mind exaggerating the truth to make it a little more exciting. If ever a girl was cut out to work for *In Touch* magazine one day, it's her.

"Hey, that's just what I heard," Amy says, pursing her lips. "Know what else? I hear everybody at the party is going to get a free iTunes gift card, and one person will get an iPod nano in the goody bag! I think that's why all the guys are here. I already saw Tommy Newman, Derek Marte, Jimmy Morehouse—"

"Jimmy's here?" you croak, your throat suddenly dry.

Jessie elbows you in the side, meaning *Shake it off fast, unless you want blabbermouth Amy to know that you have a big ol' crush on him, which you totally don't . . . right?*

"I mean, Jimmy's here?" you manage to say in a normal voice.

"He sure is! Can you believe it?" Amy says excitedly, pleased that some part of her gossip has caused a stir. "Just goes to show you how sweet this party is going to be. It even brought super-shy Jimmy out of hiding!" Before Amy can go on, her cell beeps with an incoming text message. She flips open her RAZR phone and reads the screen, her eyes widening. "Omigod, Sanjay says somebody just spotted Shawna at Sephora. Gotta go!" With that, Amy flies toward the escalators, stopping to tell everyone she meets on the way what she just heard.

"See?" Jessie cries. "Told ya so. Shawna's already been spotted. We're already off to a bad start!"

Lena, always the levelheaded one, touches Jessie's shoulder. "Calm down! We're not out of this yet. But it might be a good idea to get a little insurance. As long as we're wandering around the mall, why don't we buy the birthday girl a present, just in case we find her but get the answer to her question wrong?"

"Hmmm . . . ," you say, rubbing your chin with your thumb and index finger. "A little shameless bribery? Hey, couldn't hurt!"

Five stores later, you still haven't seen any sign of Shawna, and Jessie has started losing her mind.

"Which ones?" she is now asking Lena as you stand at the custom-jewelry kiosk next to Starbucks. "These or these?" Jessie holds up two practically identical sets of silver hoop earrings.

"Um . . . ," Lena says, nervously biting her lip. "What's the difference?"

Jessie's eyes widen in shock. "What's the difference? What do you mean what's the difference? These are a little bit thicker, but these are way bigger. See?" She lines up the two sets of earrings so that Lena can see the fraction-of-an-inch difference between them.

"Ohhh," Lena says, "now I see. Sure." Lena shoots you a look like *Get the straitjacket ready while I keep this nut job occupied.* "In that case, I'd go with this pair." She points to the ones on the left.

"Okay," Jessie says. "But are these earrings something a twelve-year-old or a *thirteen*-year-old would wear?"

Lena just smacks her own forehead and sighs. Jessie has been asking you both the same question through several stores now. Would a thirteen-year-old buy this poster or that poster? Would a thirteen-year-old get the Chunky Monkey or the Phish Food ice cream? Would a thirteen-year-old buy the cherry blossom lip gloss or the ice berry dream lip gloss? She is now officially driving you both crazy!

So far on the list of things that are preteen (and therefore donezo) are Hello Kitty stuff, red tights, David Archuleta CDs, and, apparently, slightly smaller silver hoop earrings. On the official teen-approved list are black leggings, all things *Twilight* and Robert Pattinson, Death Cab for Cutie downloads, and the Sonic Death Monkey body wash from Lush.

The list goes on, but you're too tired to think about it. Poor Lena is still being grilled and is looking to you for help.

"Don't ask me," you declare before Jessie has a chance to turn her attention to you. "I won't be thirteen for months, so I have no idea what a thirteen-year-old would like."

You smile good-naturedly at your friends and drift over to the kiosk with all the crazy hats. *Does anyone ever actually buy these giant Dr. Seuss hats?* you wonder. You wouldn't be caught dead in one. Not only would it give you the most heinous case of hat hair, but it would hide half your face! You'd have to get a Seeing Eye dog to lead you around. But those newsboy hats—now, *those* are kind of cute. You half-heartedly try on the plaid one and are checking yourself out in the mirror when suddenly you feel a tap on your shoulder. Jessie and Lena are still three kiosks down, arguing about whether a thirteen-year-old would wear a charm bracelet, so you know the shoulder-tapper isn't one of them. It has got to be the wireless-cell-phone guy again. Doesn't he ever give up? You're a pretty patient girl, but really, enough is enough. It's time to sing soprano right into this guy's face. You whip around, fully prepared to let him have it. "I said *noooo* —" you start bellowing, but quickly cut yourself off when you realize that the person tapping your shoulder is *so* not the cell-phone guy. Oops.

Instead, you're faced by a woman who looks almost as annoyed as you felt a second ago. Her jet-black hair, which perfectly matches her black T-shirt and supertight black pants, is pulled back in the world's tightest ponytail. She's got on one of those headsets with the little speaker part pointing at her mouth. You think that either this lady is from New York or she's a ninja. Either way she could probably kick your butt. *Quick—do some damage control.* "Oh! Uh . . . sorry, um, I, uh, thought you were . . . 'cause this guy with the phones . . . and I already have . . . but you're not . . . um . . ." Smooth. Real smooth.

She rolls her eyes and kind of waves your words away with her hands like they're pesky flies. "Enough," she says quickly. "Just listen."

You're not about to say no to that after the way you screamed in this innocent bystander's face. Besides, in your mind you're running through the other types of people who might like to wear all black: CIA operative? Police detective? Mime? Nun? All the possibilities are equally frightening.

"I'm a model scout," the lady says, as if she has just read your mind. (And you didn't even put "psychic" on the list!) "Have you ever done any modeling?"

"Who, me?" you squeak. "Yeah, right." Sure, you're a big-time model. That's why you spent almost every minute of the last week of your summer vacation at the very glamorous downtown mall, checking out assorted headbands and stuffing your face with Johnny Rockets sundaes.

"Well, would you like to do some modeling today? Bebe LaRue is coming out with a young-adult line of clothing and we really need a girl around your age for the photo shoot." She's smiling, but something about it seems fake, like she has to struggle to be nice and smiling kind of hurts her face.

"Are you serious?" you ask skeptically.

She abruptly drops the smile and sighs. "Look, I don't normally troll the mall looking for untrained models. But Alexa's agent called at the last minute to tell me she'd been double-booked, which means I'm in a bind." She looks you up and down quickly like she's checking out a new refrigerator or something. She does a final once-over and you apparently pass the test. "You'll do in a pinch. So? In or out? Time is money."

"In!" Jessie suddenly screams from beside you. Huh? Where did she come from?

"Yeah, she's definitely in," Lena says on the other side of you. *Wha . . . ?* Was she there a second ago?

"Thanks, girls," the headset lady says. "But I need to hear it from her." She looks right at you, but you're still speechless and unsure, which seems to annoy her. "Not that I should need to convince you—really, a million girls would kill for this offer—but if you do it, I'll pay you Alexa's usual rate for the day. And since her agent couldn't be bothered to inform me ahead of time that she would not make it today, I see no reason why I should save a spot for either one of them at the Bebe LaRue wrap party at the new Graphic Art Museum, which opens next week. Therefore, if you do well today, the two passes are yours. So do you want to be a model or not? I don't have all day."

Most boring place on earth, my eye! So far it looks like the mall is the place to be. It's not even noon yet and already you've found out that you're a big part of your friend's secret blog, you've got a shot at scoring tickets to the party of the year, there has been a confirmed Jimmy Morehouse sighting, and you could be in a Bebe LaRue photo shoot! Plus, if you do well, you get two passes to the new Graphic Art Museum—which would give you the perfect excuse to talk to Jimmy. How sick is that? But are you really willing to risk it all to be part of the fun? Or would you rather have a safety net installed before you jump off the cliff? Take the quiz and find out . . . if you dare.

QUIZ TIME!

Circle your answers and tally up the points at the end.

1. You're at an amusement park with your friends and they're all dying to get on the most insane-looking roller coaster in the place. You:
   A. hightail it to the Skee-Ball lanes, where it's safe. I mean, what are they, crazy?
   B. tell them you'd join them but somebody has to stay behind and hold everybody's bags. Plus, no one will believe they even got on the ride unless you snap a few pictures as they go whizzing by.
   C. agree to get on the ride, but only if one of your friends will let you clutch her arm in a viselike grip the whole time.

Hopefully she won't mind all the shrieking you'll be doing right in her ear.

D. make sure you're the first in line so you can sit right up front. Danger is your middle name! It'll be scary, but if you live, it'll be worth the adrenaline rush.

2. **You've had long hair since you were a kid and are kind of itching for a change. So when you go to the salon and the cool stylist with the blue hair suggests you cut it all off and go short, you:**

A. freak out. What if you cut off all your long locks, and instead of looking like Victoria Beckham, you end up looking like Edward Scissorhands? No way. You leave without even letting her touch your precious tresses.

B. tell her you would but picture day is coming up at school, and any beauty magazine worth its salt would say not to do anything extreme to your hair before an important event like that. You'll stick to your usual—a little trim—thank you very much.

C. meet her more than halfway and opt for an edgy bob that hangs just below your ears. At least your hair will still be long enough to pull back into a ponytail if it looks hideous.

D. go for it. Angelina Jolie, Natalie Portman, and Halle Berry have all rocked the short look at some point. Why not you?

3. **Your math teacher has presented the class with a doozy of a problem and is waiting for volunteers to work it out on the board. You:**

A. raise your hand . . . to go to the bathroom. You don't have to go, but hopefully by the time you get back, your teacher will have tortured some other poor sucker into solving it.

B. keep your butt firmly planted in your seat and pray that your teacher doesn't appoint a "volunteer." You don't know for sure that your answer is right, so why risk being wrong and humiliating yourself in front of the whole class?

C. volunteer, but only after comparing your answer with that of one of your classmates who is too scared to get up there in front of everyone. His answer is the same as yours, so you're a little more willing to risk public embarrassment.

D. raise your hand as high as it'll go. You aren't sure you've got the right answer, but if it means extra credit, you'll give it a shot.

4. **You're lucky enough to be selected for a game show on which you could win enough cash to buy a whole new wardrobe and a lifetime supply of music downloads. You're in the bonus round and you can choose how much of your winnings you want to bet. You:**

A. walk away. You've already won enough to earn you bragging rights at school for a year and at least three new outfits. Why take a chance on going home with nothing?

B. bet 10 percent of your winnings. If you lose, you won't have to part with much of your jackpot. And if you win, you can use the extra cash to buy a nice headband or something.

C. bet 90 percent of your winnings. If you win, you'll win big, and if you lose . . . well, at least you'll have enough left over to buy yourself plenty of paper bags to cover your head with for the rest of the school year.

D. bet it all! Go big or go home, right? Sure, you might lose, but if you win, you're in the money!

5. **The cute boy from school you want to invite to your party is standing in the hallway with a group of his friends. This might be your last chance to ask him. You:**

A. cruise by the group of boys . . . and keep on walking, making sure to avoid all eye contact. You'd rather not risk getting laughed at by his whole crew.

B. have one of your friends walk with you past the group of boys while talking WAY TOO LOUDLY ABOUT WHAT A GREAT PARTY YOU'RE HAVING THIS WEEKEND, stressing that you'll be serving what you happen to know is his favorite junk food. Then "accidentally" drop an invite on the floor near them. Hopefully he'll get the hint.

C. hand your crush an invite . . . and give one to everyone he's with too. His friends are kind of obnoxious goons and you hope they don't come, but it's the only way to invite him without making it look like you singled him out.

D. march right up to him and hand him an invitation. The worst he can do is say no.

Give yourself 1 point for every time you answered ***A***, 2 points for every ***B***, 3 points for every ***C***, and 4 points for every ***D***.

—If you scored between 5 and 12, go to page 21.

—If you scored between 13 and 20, go to page 33.

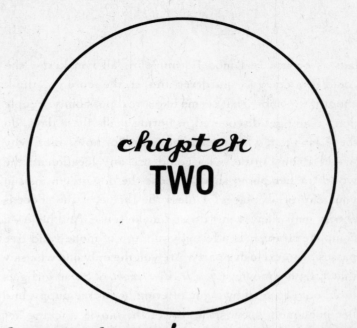

chapter
TWO

Congratulations! You have managed to successfully avoid any major risks in your life and as a result are still in one piece. You may not always choose the most exciting option, but you definitely make sure you protect yourself, which is kind of a relief to your friends and family, who rarely have to bail you out of a bad situation. Still, it might be fun to take a chance every now and then.

Do you want to be a model? Well, duh! You didn't TiVo the last three seasons of *America's Next Top Model* for nothing. Who wouldn't want to model? Free clothes, cool people, traveling all over the world . . . and did you mention the free clothes? But still, who says this lady is even a real model scout? For all you know, she could be a crazy ax murderer. In fact, the more you think about it, the more that seems like a real possibility. People don't really get discovered in boring malls these days, do they? Isn't that what reality shows are for now? Plus, why would Bebe LaRue, who could use any location in the world for her photo shoot, choose the downtown mall in your city of all places? Unless the theme of the shoot is cheesy mall glam, it just doesn't make sense. And hello—a complete stranger is offering you a ton of money and free passes to an exclusive party. Are you the only one who saw that Lifetime movie *Where Is My Daughter?* Some girl gets lured out of a mall by a guy offering her a free puppy, and her poor mom spends the rest of the movie tracking her down. She finds her alive but all muddy and gross in the woods. *So* not for you.

You try to signal to your friends with your eyes that maybe you should all make a break for it. But Jessie is bouncing up and down, smiling a big goofy smile, and Lena is busy tapping away at her BlackBerry, no doubt updating her blog to include this interesting turn of events. Usually you three seem to be able to read one another's minds, but your powers of telepathy must be on the fritz. You'll get no help from these two.

The headset lady has already started to walk off, clearly expecting you to follow her, and Jessie and Lena are gently nudging you forward. But wait just a minute!

"Whoa, whoa, whooooa . . . ," you say, and stop dead in your tracks. "I, um, need to ask my mom if it's okay first." Good thinking. And not altogether a lie either.

Headset lady rolls her eyes again and sighs. "Well, of course I'll need to speak with your mother. We do need her written consent, since you're a minor, after all. But that's what my assistant is for. He'll take care of drawing up all the necessary paperwork."

"But what if my mom says no?"

The scout just gives you a smug grin. "No one says no to me." The look on your face must scream, *You haven't met my mom, lady,* because she rolls her eyes yet again and mutters something about dealing with amateurs. "Fine. Go ask your mother first. But take this with you." She pulls a business card from her back pocket and hands it to you. "There's my contact info in case she has any questions. But you need to decide fast. Be at the Photo Hut on the second floor in twenty minutes sharp or we'll find someone else." With that, she stalks off, talking quickly into her headset to somebody named Steve.

When you finally look at your friends, they are both staring at you with their jaws on the floor. "Are you crazy?" Jessie is the first to yell. "You just got discovered by a major talent scout and you're saying no? We're talking about a shot at modeling the Bebe LaRue line here. Do you seriously not know how big that is? Perez mentions her in his blog all the time!"

You look to Lena to back you up, since she's usually the voice of reason. But she's shaking her head in disappointment too. "Sorry, but Jessie's right. Even I would do it! I don't know how much they were planning to pay Alexa, but I'm betting it would be enough to cover at least a year's worth of books in college. Not to mention that modeling would be an amazing extracurricular to list on your résumé."

"Lena," you deadpan, "I'm twelve. I don't *have* a résumé yet."

"Yes, well, all the more reason to do it. Besides, did you not hear where she said the wrap party would be? At the new Graphic Art Museum! It hasn't even opened yet, and I bet a certain comic-book geek—"

"Hey, can you guys stop calling him a geek?" you interrupt.

"Of course, lovebird. Sorry. What I meant to say was, I bet a certain *artist* would love to get an early peek at that museum. If you were able to get into that party, no way could he say no if you invited him."

There Lena goes again, making all kinds of sense.

"Sure, I know. It would be awesome!" you agree. "But I'm not walking away with some stranger. How do we know that scout is who she says she is? We've gotta check her out first, that's all."

"Fair enough," Lena says, swayed by your logic. "What do you suggest?"

"Follow me," you order, waving them forward. "We're

heading for the Internet café. After all, what is Google for if not a situation like this, right?"

"Right!" Jessie agrees. "Well, this and getting a closer look at what everybody wore to the Kids' Choice Awards. But let's get a move on. You haven't got much time. And you don't want to keep all those glam models waiting!"

After three minutes of navigating through the crowds of bored-looking teenagers and tired moms pushing strollers, the three of you arrive at the Internet café and pay for thirty minutes of computer time. You quickly log on and type the name on the headset lady's card—Janice Iverson— into the Google search line. In a flash, a long list of hits comes up. All have Janice's name in bold. First you read the Wikipedia entry, which confirms that not only is Janice a model scout, but she is *the* model scout. Even though she's only in her midthirties, she is responsible for having put half the models in the Calvin Klein ads on the map. She's the one all the major designers turn to when they need fresh new faces. She got divorced from her CEO husband a few years ago and now plans to start her own agency. She has even started directing her own magazine ads and TV commercials. The friends list on her MySpace page is like a Who's Who of the fashion industry—the most notable entry being Bebe LaRue herself! It turns out that LaRue is from your hometown. There's even a recent picture of her accepting the key to the city from your mayor, and Janice is standing in the background.

"I was wondering why in the world a famous designer would have a fashion shoot in this Podunk town. Now it makes sense! It's her way of giving back to the place where she got her start."

"See that?" Jessie gushes. "There's hope for us yet!"

Scrolling through the other Web links, you find pictures of Janice and Tyra Banks, Janice and Ashton Kutcher, Janice and the entire cast of *Gossip Girl* . . . "Oh. My. God. She is the real deal!" you say, amazed.

"Exactly!" Jessie shouts. "So you're gonna do it, right? You should totally do it."

Lena nods in agreement and claps her hands together. "Yea, verily."

"But what about the golden tickets?" you ask Jessie. "You'll be down one Oompa-Loompa to help you search the chocolate factory—"

"Would you shut up about the party and get out of here?" Jessie cuts you off.

"Yeah," Lena says. "We'll text you if there are any Shawna sightings. Go forth and be fabulous. Just remember while you're hanging with the glamazons: to thine own-self be true."

"Um . . . Justin Timberlake?" you joke.

"Very funny, you lunkhead."

"And text us if there are any cute model boys at the shoot that we should see," Jessie adds, her blue eyes twinkling.

"You guys are the greatest," you say. "Okay, I'll do it! One of you call my mom and let her know, okay? And give her Janice's number." You hand Janice's card to Jessie. "Now, just let me log out and . . . Oh no!" When you notice the clock at the top of the computer screen, you see that you've spent so much time online that your twenty minutes are almost up. You've blown it already! There's no way you'll make it to the Photo Hut in four minutes. Your friends notice the time too.

"Uh-oh," Lena says. "Looks like it's time to put those long legs of yours to good use. *Run!*"

Without another word, you bolt out of your chair and fly out of the Internet café. But just as you're rounding that first bend, you run right smack into some guy and totally wipe out in the middle of the mall. Ouch! Not your most graceful moment. As you're lying there staring up at the fluorescent lights, your head pounding slightly now, you think this is not a good start to your modeling career—assaulting someone on the way to your first shoot. Worse yet, that little crash landing just shaved another thirty seconds off the amount of time you had left to get to the Photo Hut, so you are seriously considering making this a hit-and-run.

But the non-jerky side of you (which, fortunately, is way bigger than your jerky side) decides that you should at least make sure your victim is okay. By the time you finally ease your way onto your feet and walk over to the figure on the floor, he is sitting up with his face turned down, rubbing his forehead, where it looks like a huge knot is developing. You hold out your hand to help him up, and say, "I'm *so* sorry about that. Are you all right?"

And when he looks up at you, you finally see who it is: Jimmy Morehouse, in all his disheveled glory.

His dark green eyes widen a little when he sees you.

It could just be the bump on your own head, but you think Jimmy seems nervous.

"I—I'll live . . . uh, I think," he stammers, dusting off his PICASSO IS MY HOMEBOY T-shirt. Never has he seemed more crushworthy—even though his floppy brown hair now looks like he just got hit by lightning. "Going somewhere in a hurry?" he asks, grinning a little.

You're pretty sure that is the longest sentence he's ever said to you. And his grin kind of makes you want to stay in the hallway with him for the rest of the day, but time is *tick-tick-tick*ing away.

Can you handle this? The model scout is who she says she is, and not an insane kidnapping ax murderer, your friends prove how awesome they are by being crazy supportive, and you've just run right into Jimmy (literally, unfortunately)! The question is, will you listen to your head (which is telling you to go live out your modeling dream) or your heart (which is telling you to stay put right where you are with Jimmy, your full-on crush)? There's only one way to know for sure. Take the quiz to find out!

QUIZ TIME!

Circle your answers and tally up the points at the end.

1. **If you were stranded on a desert island with just a DVD player and three movies to watch forever, you would bring:**

   A. *When Harry Met Sally, The Notebook, 50 First Dates.* Those are a few of the most romantic movies you've ever seen, and you could spend a lifetime (or however long you're stuck on that island) watching the characters fall in love. Swoon . . .

   B. *Spider-Man 3, Harry Potter and the Half-Blood Prince, Pirates of the Caribbean: At World's End.* Those movies have plenty of adventure and you're a sucker for superheroes, wizards, and pirates, but the love stories between Peter Parker and Mary Jane Watson, Harry Potter and Ginny Weasley, and of course Will Turner and Elizabeth Swann are what really drive the action.

   C. *WALL-E, The Fast and the Furious: Tokyo Drift, The Dark Knight.* Sure, there's a touch of romance in all those movies, but the real focus is on awesome space adventures, fast cars, and dangerous villains—just the way you like it!

   D. *Friday the 13th, Shaun of the Dead, Iron Man.* Who needs sappy love stories when you can have zombies, a deranged killer in a hockey mask, and one of the coolest comic-book heroes ever? Bring on the fight scenes!

2. **The night of your friend's sleepover is also your parents' anniversary, and they have planned a romantic evening of dinner at a fancy French bistro and dancing under the stars. But at the last minute the babysitter calls to say she has the flu, so she can't watch your little brother. You:**

A. cancel your plans immediately and agree to stay home and babysit. Nothing should get in the way of your folks' having a beautiful candlelit dinner together at a swanky restaurant. There will be other sleepovers.

B. offer to babysit, but subtly encourage your parents not to stay out too late. If they get home early enough, maybe they'd be willing to drop you off at your friend's house in time for the "slumber" portion of the slumber party.

C. agree to babysit, but drop a lot of not-so-subtle hints about how much you were looking forward to the slumber party. Nothing like a good guilt trip to get your parents to reschedule.

D. try to tiptoe out of the house before your 'rents even realize you're still there. You've had these plans forever and no way are you missing out on all the fun. Besides, it's just dinner. What's the big deal?

3. **If you could be on any reality show, you would choose:**

A. *The Bachelor.* They always choose a major dreamboat to be the bachelor, and how romantic would it be to receive the final rose and be proposed to on the beach in front of the whole world?

B. *Beauty and the Geek.* Okay, so you probably wouldn't be paired with your ideal guy, but you firmly believe that there is a little beauty and a little geek in all of us. Plus, if you win, you split a bunch of cool prizes!

C. *So You Think You Can Dance.* Not only would you learn how to do really beautiful couples dances, like the waltz and the tango, but you could win a ton of money, go on tour, and be considered America's favorite dancer!

D. *Amazing Race.* You can see it now: you and your BFF traveling to exotic places, like Morocco and China, following clues, performing crazy tasks, and doing your best to outsmart the other teams. Talk about exciting!

4. **The guy your best friend likes is moving away and she is heart-broken. How do you comfort her?**

A. By telling her that you're sure if the two of them are meant to be, they will meet again somehow. And in the meantime, think of all the romantic letters they can send each other!

B. By taking her to your older brother's baseball practice. There will be a lot of boys there, and it might help your friend realize that there are other fish in the sea.

C. You let her vent, then try to distract her by inviting her to your house for a marathon of all the scariest nonromantic movies you can think of. A little *Halloween,* anyone?

D. You tell her to move on and think about something else. He's just a boy, after all. Why sit around crying over him when you could be playing soccer or riding your bikes in the park?

5. **It's your aunt's birthday and you're trying to pick out a card. Which one do you go with?**

A. The really sappy one with the long poem about what a great aunt she is. You would never say that stuff to her face, but that's how you feel, and you know she'll be touched.

B. The one that has a single flower on the front and just says "Happy Birthday." Inside you write a brief personal message telling her you love her. It's simple and elegant and gets right to the point.

C. The funny one with the barrel of monkeys inside. The best birthday present you can think of is a big belly laugh.

D. You decide cards are too cheesy. You'll just wish her a happy birthday when you see her. No need to get all mushy about it.

Give yourself 1 point for every time you answered **A**, 2 points for every **B**, 3 points for every **C**, and 4 points for every **D**.

—If you scored between 5 and 12, turn to page 48.
—If you scored between 13 and 20, turn to page 60.

chapter THREE

Sweet! Looks like you are a real go-getter! Your friends might think you're off your rocker sometimes, but you know that you're just living life to the fullest. You are determined not to let silly fears get in the way of doing things that are exciting. Every day for you is one big adventure! But do your friends and family a favor and look before you leap, Ms. Daredevil. Even skydivers make sure they've got extra parachutes.

Do you want to be a model? Well, duh! You didn't TiVo the last three seasons of *America's Next Top Model* for nothing. Who wouldn't want to model? Free clothes, cool people, traveling all over the world . . . and did you mention the free clothes?

Before the scout has a chance to change her mind, you cry, "Let's go!" Whoops! Almost forgot your friends and why you were at the mall to begin with. "I'm so sorry I won't be able to help you find Shawna, but you guys understand, right?"

"Are you mental? Of course we understand!" Jessie insists.

"Yeah, just keep your Sidekick handy in case we have any Shawna updates," Lena adds. "And remember: 'Be not afraid of greatness: some are born great, some achieve greatness, and some have greatness thrust upon them.'"

"Hmmm . . . wise words," Jessie says. "Paris Hilton?" She grins at you. You both love messing with Lena this way, since you know it drives her crazy.

Lena rolls her eyes. "Hardly. It's from *Twelfth Night*."

You and Jessie give her a blank stare.

"You know, Shakespeare?"

Jessie shrugs. "Never heard of 'im. Has he been in any movies I might have seen? Or does he have a reality show coming out on VH1?"

"Ugh, you're hopeless," Lena says, catching on. She gives Jessie a playful shove, then turns back to you, smiling sheepishly. "It's just my way of saying good luck. Now go achieve some greatness!"

"I'll try," you say, and hug them both. Then you turn to the mysterious ninja. "All right, I'm ready!"

"Finally," headset lady says. "By the way, my name is Janice Iverson." Good. Now you can stop calling her "headset lady." She shakes your hand and quickly examines your fingernails. Thank goodness you gave yourself a manicure the day before. Janice nods curtly at you and then touches her hand to her headset. "Steve? Yeah. I've got one. Get the clothes laid out and have the consent forms ready to fax to her guardian. We're on our way. Be there in four minutes."

And just like that, the two of you are off and running. Well, *you're* running. Janice just seems to be making these long strides, like a giraffe. You have to take three or four steps for every one of hers, but you don't care. You're on your way to a real-life photo shoot! How awesome is that?

Janice has barely hung up from her call with Steve when her phone rings again. "What is it now?" she barks. "What do you mean Natasha fell off her stilettos and her leg is broken? Unacceptable! I don't care how long the hospital wants to keep her there. I'm already being forced to make do with an amateur for the LaRue shoot." She steals a backward glance at you. "I don't really have time to audition more girls for the face-wash commercial. So unless Natasha's leg has actually fallen off, she'd better show up!" Janice slams the phone shut and you can practically see the steam coming out of her ears. Scary!

When you get to the Photo Hut, everything is a little surreal. This is the same place where families go to make cheesy holiday postcards. There is usually a crying baby in the corner, posing with a giant beach ball or something. And there are all these completely fake-looking backgrounds, like the sky with perfect white clouds, or big trees with red and orange leaves falling. But not today. All that stuff has been covered up with crisp white sheets, and instead of the little old man who usually works the camera, trying to get toddlers to smile by shaking a Dora the Explorer doll at them, there are three or four youngish photographers pacing around, setting up lights and what look like huge umbrellas. You have to admit, it's a lot classier than usual, but still . . . why would they choose this place as a location when they could have done the shoot in Paris, Milan, or New York City? The first kernel of doubt enters your mind. Is this thing for real?

Just then you spot a row of director's chairs to your left, where the other models are getting their hair blown out and teased. You're pretty sure you've seen at least two of them in Delia's catalogs. And is that the guy from the Abercrombie & Fitch ads? Just like that, the kernel of doubt pops. This is real, all right! After Steve takes care of faxing your mom the consent forms—which she agrees to sign (phew!)—you are ushered to the right side, where there is another director's chair and a huge brightly lit mirror. "Sheila!" Janice barks. "This one needs makeup, pronto!"

A harried-looking brunette woman comes flying out from behind a white curtain, carrying what looks like a tackle box. "I'm on it," she tells Janice, who strides away, yelling, "Steve! Are those clothes ready?"

Sheila shakes her head at Janice's back. "I swear, she's gonna give herself an ulcer one of these days. Hi, I'm Sheila, and you must be our brand-new model. Well, welcome aboard. Is this your first time? Sure, of course it is. I can tell by the condition of your face. You don't moisturize, do you? You've got to learn to moisturize every night. It's never too soon to start practicing good skin-care habits. I mean, look at me. How old would you say I am? Thirty-one? Thirty-three tops, right? Well, I'm forty-six! I know! Hard to believe, isn't it? It's all about the skin. We used to give all the models deep-cleaning facials before the shoots, but with the budget cuts and all . . . Ooh, don't tell anyone I said that. Ms. LaRue doesn't like to acknowledge that even she's had to cut back. I mean, why else would we be shooting at—no offense—this tacky Photo Hut? Sure, she'll tell you it's because this month marks the anniversary of when she launched her fashion line and since she's from this town and actually used to work in this dump, she wanted to honor the place where she got her start, but between you and me . . . she just wanted to save a few bucks. I guess the good ol' days of jetting off to Saint-Tropez at a moment's notice are gone." Sheila heaves a deep sigh. "But anyway, where was I? Oh, right. Proper skin care . . ."

The whole time Sheila is talking, she is rubbing foundation onto your face, pulling a pencil across your eyebrows, and running a finger dabbed with pink lipstick across your lips. She hasn't let you get a word in edgewise, but that's fine, since you really wouldn't know what to say anyway. The whole thing feels like a weird dream. You're sitting here having your makeup done by a professional, and someone is scrambling in the back to get your wardrobe together. It's like you're at some fancy event in an area where only VIPs are allowed—and for once, that means *you*!

"Helloooo, earth to New Girl," Sheila is saying, snapping her fingers in front of your face. "Wake up. Your makeup is done. Head over to hair. Chop-chop."

"Right . . . sorry. I m-mean, thanks," you stammer. You rush to the other bank of chairs, and before you even settle back in your seat, there are a brush in your hair and a blow dryer whirring over your head. The man doing the styling is asking you questions too, probably about your split ends, but you can't hear him, so you just keep saying, "What? What?" He gives up and continues his work in silence. It normally takes you almost an hour to get your hair whipped into something that resembles a style, but this guy is done in a matter of minutes. He spins the chair around so that you are facing the mirror, and you are totally shocked by what you see. Between the makeup and the glammed-up do, you barely recognize yourself. It's you, but a way chicer version of you. Wow!

But these must be some kind of trick mirrors, because along with your own reflection, you can see what looks like the image of the new girl from school, Mona Winston, the biggest brat ever. You haven't known each other that long, but somehow you've already gotten on her bad side—probably because the first time you met her, you accidentally stepped on her exclusive Christian Louboutin ballerina flats, leaving a barely noticeable scuff mark. It was an accident, but she thought you did it on purpose, and has been making your life miserable ever since. (Although you have a feeling she would have tried to make your life miserable even if the incident had never happened. That's just how she is.) You almost rub your eyes to clear up this horrible illusion, but you suspect that Sheila would cut off your head if you ruined her makeup job. Instead, you close your eyes for a moment, hoping that when you open them, Mona will be gone and you can assume that her appearance was a bad hallucination. But when you open them, there she is again, getting fitted for a LaRue masterpiece. You heard from Amy that Mona has done some modeling — which would explain her mysterious frequent absences from class — but you just never believed it. So really, what is she doing here?

And what you only thought, Mona says out loud, glaring your way.

"What are *you* doing here?"

She stomps over to you, her face all scrunched up like she just ate a bagful of lemons. The hairstylist takes one look at Mona's pouty face, throws his hands up in surrender, and backs away. *Don't panic. You can handle this,* you tell yourself.

"Hey, Mona," you say, managing to sound friendly. "Looks like Janice needed one more person to rock some of the outfits today and I was in the right place at the right time. Who knows? Maybe one day I'll be strutting down the runway right next to you!" you gush excitedly.

"Not if I have anything to say about it," Mona snaps. "*I'm* the star of this show!"

What is her problem? you think. But there's no time to find out. Just then Janice stalks into the room, tugging at your arm. "Steve, this one is done with hair and makeup. Take her to the back and show her the clothes she'll be wearing. Mona, go finish your fitting. I'd like to get this shoot started sometime this year!"

"Fine," Mona says huffily. Then, under her breath so only you can hear, she mutters, "This isn't over."

You try to ignore her as Steve, a college-aged guy with his short hair cut into a sort of mini Mohawk, leads you to the back room and shows you a brown leather garment bag. "These are your clothes. Don't tug at anything, don't rip anything, and, for goodness' sake, don't spill anything on them."

"You forgot to tell her not to roll around in mud or get into a food fight while wearing the precioussss," a voice adds sarcastically from the corner, saying the last part like Gollum in *The Lord of the Rings*.

You glance over to see a bored-looking kid around your age. He barely looks up from his PSP game to acknowledge you. He's definitely a gamer. He's wearing a large dark blue T-shirt over a long-sleeved white top and a pair of ripped jeans. (Jessie the fashionista would tell you that the proper term is "distressed," but who are we kidding? Those jeans are crying for mercy!) He has a skateboard propped against his chair, and his messy dirty-blond hair is hanging over one eye in a way that seems both careless and perfect at the same time. You feel a little guilty for thinking this, since you promised Jessie and Lena you would finally get up the nerve to talk to Jimmy today, but this mystery guy is a major cutie.

Steve sighs, clearly exasperated. "Gee, thanks, bro," he says with mock sincerity. "Always the little helper, aren't you?" Steve turns back to you and says, "Don't mind him. That's just my little brother, Bryan."

At the mention of his name, Bryan raises a hand and says, "Hey." You respond with a nod and a slight smile, hoping the gesture looks at least a little cool.

"I promised to drop him off at the arcade after the shoot, but it's taking longer than expected, so he's getting a little cranky, aren't you, cranky pants?" Steve calls over his shoulder.

"Whatever," Bryan says, stealing another glance at you.

"For the record," Steve continues, "um, don't roll around in mud and don't get into any food fights while wearing these clothes, get it?"

"Aw, there go my plans for the afternoon," you say dryly. Steve gives you a stern look. "I mean, got it." You nod seriously. Out of the corner of your eye, you can see Bryan smile a little, though he's pretending not to listen.

"Good. Now, where in the world did I put those gold flats?" Steve says, checking around the room in a panic.

"Can't I just wear the shoes I have on?" you offer. Steve whirls around and looks from your beat-up old Nikes to you. Nikes, you. Nikes, you. He cocks one eyebrow and kind of smirks, like *You're kidding, right?* Okay, guess not.

"I'll go find the shoes. Take those *things* off and hide them somewhere and pray Janice doesn't notice them. Better yet, burn them. And you"—he points to Bryan—"take your PSP in the other room like a good little monster and give the lady some privacy."

Bryan gets up from his chair with an exaggerated sigh. "That's my big brother—always bossing me around." He gives you a quick nod. "See you later." And it could just be your ears playing tricks on you, but you could swear that he mumbled under his breath, "I hope."

As soon as they leave, you open the bag and almost squeal with delight when you see the clothes. You try not to giggle as you pull on a royal blue eyelet dress with a scooped neck and a chunky leather belt around the waist. Then you slide into the cropped jacket that goes with it, careful not to ruin your makeup. Checking yourself out in the mirror, you admire the way the dress flares out a little when you twirl. You love it! Just then you remember that you haven't checked your Sidekick in a while. You click it open, wondering if Jessie and Lena have made any progress, but you're not getting any reception back here. So you tiptoe out of the room, bare feet and all, when suddenly you hear whispering on the other side of the curtain.

"I don't really care what you want, young lady. This is your job."

That was definitely Janice. You've known her for only about an hour, but already you'd recognize that ice-cold tone anywhere.

"But, Moooom," a whiny voice replies, "it's so not fair!"

Hey, that's Mona! But wait a minute. Did she just call Janice Mom? Hmmm . . . this could be interesting.

And the plot thickens, as they say. You've taken the plunge and found yourself on a real-life high-fashion photo shoot (your dream!) only to be confronted with bad cell reception and your archnemesis, Mona (your nightmare). Meeting Bryan has softened the blow of that unpleasant surprise a little—especially since you haven't seen Jimmy yet—but you're still going to have to deal with Ms. Star of the Show to have any hope of doing well today and scoring those passes to the wrap party. Listening in on this convo between Mona and Janice (Did she really call her Mom?) could be the key. And let's face it: you're just curious. Still, are you the kind of person to eavesdrop? Not sure? Looks like you'd better take the quiz to find out.

QUIZ TIME!
Circle your answers and tally up the points at the end.

1. You're home alone when you happen to notice that your little sister left her diary open on the kitchen table. Something has definitely been up with her lately. So you:

A. read it from cover to cover. You wouldn't call that snooping—you're just a concerned older sister. If she's not going to tell you what's wrong, you have to find out somehow, right?

B. "accidentally" read a few pages just to get the gist. You reason that her choice of red pen was a cry for help and she probably wanted you to read those pages anyway. (That's your story and you're sticking to it.)

C. close the diary without reading a word, but vow to grill her about what's been going on with her as soon as she gets home. If she won't talk to you voluntarily, maybe she needs a little push.

D. respect her privacy and close the diary immediately. You then put it back in her room so no one else can read it either. When she's ready to talk to you about whatever's bugging her, she will.

2. **When you go to the food court with your friend, you try to sit at a table that is:**

A. right in the middle of the most crowded section. You just love hearing everybody's conversations around you. You can pick up the best gossip that way.

B. somewhere near the flat-screen TV that is always tuned in to the entertainment channel. You and your friend love to hear all the celebrity dirt and then talk about it for hours.

C. near the Johnny Rockets, where all the popular kids hang out. The queen bee of that crowd is always stirring up some sort of drama, and if you sit in the area, you'll be right there to see it. If not, you'll still have a great time downing milk shakes with your friend and talking about school.

D. at a two-seater off to the side. You love having a quiet place where you can tune everyone else out and really catch up with your buddy.

3. **You're in a bathroom stall when two other people come into the restroom, having a private conversation. You:**

   A. lift your feet so that they can't tell you're in there. Conversations that girls drag their friends into the bathroom to have are usually pretty juicy, and you've got the best seat in the house . . . so to speak.

   B. don't hide your presence, but don't exactly announce it either. Hey, it's not your fault if they don't notice you're in there. Everybody knows you're supposed to check under the stall doors for feet before you spill your guts.

   C. cough and make a lot of noise unrolling the toilet paper. You've revealed embarrassing information before when you didn't know somebody was in the stalls listening, and it made you cringe. You'd hate to make someone else feel that way.

   D. hurry up and finish your business and get out of the bathroom. It is an understood rule among girls that the bathroom confessional is sacred, and you wouldn't want to violate the code.

4. **When you go online, you:**

   A. check all your friends' MySpace and Facebook pages to see if they've added anyone new. Then you check out the pages of all those people too and Google anyone you find interesting. Then you check your Twitter account to see what your friends are up to at that precise moment. Some would call it being nosy. You say you're just thirsty for knowledge!

   B. check your Facebook page and read up on everybody's status for the day and see if any of your friends have written new notes. It's the next best thing to checking in on them in real life.

   C. check your own e-mail and maybe your horoscope. Then it's back to your homework. Running your *own* life is a full-time job. Who has the energy to monitor everyone else's?

   D. do whatever research you need to do for school, and that's about it. You check your e-mail only once or twice a week, figuring that if anything really interesting were going down, one of your friends would call to tell you. And Twittering seems like a big ol' waste of time. Do you really need to know if so-and-so is eating a cheeseburger right that second? Hardly.

5. **On your way to the library, you spot a celebrity you're a big fan of sitting alone at a table for two in a fancy outdoor café. Unbelievable! So naturally, you:**

A. hang back behind a tree and watch. You want to see what he orders. Will he go the healthy route and order a spinach salad? Or will he totally pig out and get the endless pasta plate smothered in heavy cream and cheese? And will some A-list starlet be joining him for a not-so-secret rendezvous? You've just got to know!

B. walk up to him and politely ask if it would be all right for you to bother him for his autograph. With any luck, it'll take him a while to find a pen, and while you're standing there, his mystery date will be revealed. If not, at least you'll leave with an autograph.

C. settle for using your camera phone to click a few quick pictures of your idol, then keep on heading for the library. You've heard that celebrities hate it when fans invade their personal space while they're trying to have a meal, and you don't want to be one of those pushy people.

D. keep on walking. It's cool to see a star in your hometown but you know that he's just a person and he deserves some privacy just like the rest of us. You think the paparazzi who follow him around are the biggest creeps in the world.

Give yourself 1 point for every time you answered **A**, 2 points for every **B**, 3 points for every **C**, and 4 points for every **D**.

—If you scored between 5 and 12, go to page 73.

—If you scored between 13 and 20, go to page 83.

chapter FOUR

You are a hopeless romantic. You're always first in line to help decorate for the Valentine's Day dance, and you're still heartbroken that Jennifer Aniston and Brad Pitt broke up. Some may accuse you of having your head in the clouds, but you don't care. You believe in love. Good for you! Just remember not to spend all your time daydreaming or you'll miss out on everything else.

You could very well be dreaming this, but it looks like you're sitting at a booth in Johnny Rockets with Lena, Jessie, and Jimmy Morehouse! After the two of you crashed in the hallway, your friends came running to see what happened. What they found was Jimmy holding his bruised forehead with one hand and holding your hand with the other—and Amy Choi recording the whole embarrassing scene with her video phone and forwarding it to her entire contact list. *Great,* you thought. You wouldn't be surprised if that clip showed up on YouTube tomorrow.

Lena offered to take care of Jimmy while you ran off to the shoot, but you just didn't have the heart to do that. Especially since the heart you *did* have was beating a mile a minute. So instead, you said, "Hey, let me buy you a milk shake." It was the least you could do, considering the brain damage you'd probably caused him. (Side note: You managed to utter eight whole words to him without bursting into flames! Niiice.)

He smiled shyly at you, let you pull him slowly to his feet, then shrugged and said, "Sure. Why not?" How cool is he? He wasn't even mad that you'd plowed into him like a freight train.

And now here you all are in a red leather booth, drinking your thick-as-ice-cream milk shakes and sharing a giant plate of fries while you listen to Elvis sing "All Shook Up" on the jukebox. And as Jessie fills Jimmy in on your quest to find Shawna, you could swear his sneaker is slightly touching yours under the table. There are even other kids from school here to witness this miraculous event. You already see Mary Sunshine and her best friend, Holly Happy-Go-Lucky, heading toward your table. Those aren't their real last names, obviously. It's just what people call them behind their backs, because they are the total opposite of that. If you look up "gloom" and "doom" in the dictionary, you'd see a picture of these two. They always look unbelievably bored and miserable, no matter where they are, kind of like Eeyore from those Winnie the Pooh cartoons.

"Hey," Mary says, nodding toward your group, her black shaggy hair hanging over her eyes. "You guys haven't seen Shawna yet, have you?"

"Hey, Mary," Jessie answers brightly. "No, no sightings yet."

"See?" Holly laments, looking up at Mary, who is almost five inches taller than her. "Told you this whole thing was bogus. Shawna probably just wanted to see the whole class running around the mall like morons." She rolls her eyes, then throws her head back, her long chestnut brown hair falling back to reveal a black Paramor T-shirt. "Man, what a waste of a day!"

"Yeah, we might as well have stayed home," Mary adds, kicking invisible rocks.

"Wait—so you guys *want* to go to the party?" you ask, a bit shocked. You just didn't think a party would really fit into the whole doom-and-gloom way of life.

Mary looks away nervously, as if you have caught her doing something embarrassing. "Not really," she says with a shrug. "It's just, you know, something to do. Whatev."

"Right," Lena says. "Well, don't give up yet. Amy said somebody saw Shawna at Sephora."

"Doubt it." Holly gestures with her head to Mary for them to leave. "Later."

As the two of them shuffle off, a storm cloud following their every move, you swing your eyes back to Jimmy, who is struggling to hold in a laugh. When Mary and Holly are finally gone, he lets it out, his eyes watering a little. His laugh is the greatest sound in the whole world. Like he's hiccupping and laughing at the same time. He even snorts a little! Adorable.

"Sorry," he says, wiping his eyes. "But those two are like Dementors or something! Where's a good Patronus when you need one?" Everybody at the table cracks up. Wow, he's cute *and* he's a Harry Potter fan. Who knew that Jimmy could be outgoing? When he's not being a shy, brooding artist, he's pretty funny.

As if that weren't enough, when the check comes, Jimmy insists on paying for everybody. "Nuh-uh," you object. "I'm the one who caused you internal bleeding. I should pay." You reach for the check, but he snatches it out of your reach.

"No way. The guy with the severe blood loss gets to decide who pays, so back off," he says with a smile. "Besides, you need to save your money to pay for all the stitches I'll need."

Amazing. Not only does he kind of look like Zac Efron, but he's fun, sweet, smart . . . Okay, fine. Maybe you're biased because you are definitely crushing on him. But that doesn't make it any less true. And by the way Lena and Jessie are smiling at the two of you and nudging each other, you can tell they've already given him their official stamp of approval and will no longer be calling him comic-book geek. They didn't even make a big deal about it when he accidentally tipped over the ketchup bottle and sent sticky red goo squirting across the table. If anything, that just made you like him even more. He is like your klutzy twin soul.

"I guess it turned out okay that you skipped the photo shoot after all, huh?" Jessie offers, winking at you while Jimmy is busy taking the money out of his wallet.

But at Jessie's words, his head shoots up and his eyes open as wide as saucers. "Photo shoot? You mean for Bebe LaRue?"

"Yeah," Lena says, dropping a french fry back onto the plate. "How did *you* know about that?"

All three of you are staring at him in surprise. Suddenly the super-shy Jimmy you know from school reappears. He stares down at the table and mumbles something about knowing someone at that shoot.

"Who?" you ask. "Is it your mom?"

"Your cousin?" Jessie adds.

"Your friend?" Lena asks.

Please don't let it be a girl, please don't let it be a girl. . . .

"Um . . . w-well," Jimmy stammers. "One of the models is kind of, sort of . . . my date to Shawna's party. You know Mona? Well, she already got a golden ticket weeks ago in exchange for bringing some professional photographers to the party, and each ticket admits two people, so . . . she asked me to go with her. I was actually on my way to meet her when I crashed into you." He says all this while staring down at his napkin, as if he's embarrassed. But you aren't sure if it's because he let Jessie go on and on about how much she wanted one of Shawna's tickets, never mentioning that he had one, or because he's been sort of flirting with you all this time, never mentioning that he's already Mona's date to the party.

"Oh." In case you were wondering, that crumpling sound you hear is your heart being crushed like a million old soda cans in a trash compactor. He's going with *Mona*? The one girl in school who just happens to hate your guts for no good reason? Great. So much for the romantic comedy you've been daydreaming about. No one at the table says anything for a while. All you hear is Mary Sunshine's voice in your head: *That just figures.* You guess you're not the only girl with half a brain around here. You're dying to know why he would agree to go with Mona (aka dream stealer), but your pride won't let you ask. You can only hope that your best buds can find a way to whisk you out of here ASAP (to Japan, maybe?). But they were clearly thrown off guard by Jimmy's revelation too.

Jessie is the first to recover, chirping, "Oh . . . cool!" while giving your hand a sympathetic squeeze under the table. But Lena just nervously fumbles with her Black-Berry. You make a mental note to go over some emergency evacuation drills with your BFFs. When in a horrifying, heart-crushing situation such as this, it's important to have an escape plan ready!

The silence is going from stunned to downright awkward when suddenly your cell phone rings, thank goodness. You pick it up and say hello.

"Eeeeeeee!" Amy is squealing in your ear. "Lizette just won a ticket!" Apparently Lizette had spotted Shawna posing as a mannequin in the junior miss department of Macy's. Lizette had been given a list of celebrities that she had to match to the causes they support. That was easy, in your opinion. Leonardo DiCaprio: global warming awareness. Christina Applegate: breast cancer research. Diddy: voter registration.

"And you know what else?" Amy says. (Her news always comes in twos.) "There are only a few tickets left, but it turns out each golden ticket admits two, so you can bring someone with you! Isn't that great?"

Yeah, great, you think, not bothering to tell Amy that you already heard that last piece of news. Not only have the odds of your scoring a ticket to the party gotten worse, but you missed out on a chance to be a model for Bebe LaRue, and Jimmy—who would have been your ideal date for the birthday bash—is already going with Mona. Maybe Holly was right after all. So far this has been a complete waste of a day.

Oh, bummer. Who could have seen that one coming? Both your dream of being a model and your dream of bringing Jimmy as your date to the party just went down in flames. Oh well. Happens to the best of us.

What's important is how you handle it now. Will you just roll with the punches or will you be throwing a few punches of your own (metaphorically speaking, of course)? Take the quiz to figure out what you would really do—and be honest!

QUIZ TIME!

Circle your answers and tally up the points at the end.

1. You and your family are having chocolate cake for dessert and there's only one piece left. You:

   A. hurry up and snatch the last piece. Yeah, your little bro probably wanted it too, but you can't help it if you're faster than he is!

   B. agree to share the last piece—but you do the cutting and naturally your little brother gets a tiny sliver while you give yourself the lion's share. Hey, one of the perks of being the older sibling is that you get the bigger piece of cake. He's lucky you're giving him any at all. Besides, a growing girl needs her chocolate fix! And you wouldn't want him to get cavities, right? Riiiight.

   C. do what any mature young lady such as yourself would do: flip a coin. Heads, you win; tails, your little brother loses. What's that? He doesn't fall for that one anymore? Okay, okay, you'll do a fair coin toss, and to the victor goes the chocolate cake.

   D. give the last piece to your little brother and throw in an ice-cold glass of milk. Even though he's much smaller than you, his sweet tooth is twice the size of yours.

2. Your friend has had a rotten day. She calls you, hoping you two can go out for some mint chocolate chip ice cream to get her through this rough patch. But the *America's Next Top Model* finale that you DVR'd just started. You've been way too busy to watch it before now and have been ducking spoiler Web sites for way too long. What to do?

   A. Tell her you can't go. It's too bad she had a horrible day, but you've been dying to watch this episode all week. You're sure she'll understand. You promise to call her tomorrow when you're free.

   B. Tell her she can come over to your house and watch the finale with you instead—but warn her that there is absolutely no talking allowed during the show and definitely no crying. You need quiet to focus on all of Nigel's witty observations.

   C. Tell her you'll be right over, but first you fast-forward to the end of the show and watch the last half hour just to satisfy your curiosity. You won't be able to focus on your friend at all if you're still preoccupied with the *ANTM* finale.

   D. Tell her you'll come right over. You hate to miss the show, but your pal needs you right now, and that's way more important than finding out who flopped on the CoverGirl commercial. You are fully prepared to spend the next two hours listening to her let it all out.

3. The class trip is tomorrow and it involves a one-hour bus ride. You and your best friend plan to sit next to each other and listen to music, but her iPod is broken. You offer to share yours and:

A. fill it with all the music you like. Your friend doesn't really have the same taste, but hey, it's your iPod. You wouldn't be able to stand listening to anything you don't love for a whole hour. Besides, your selections are better than hers, and one day she'll thank you for showing her what good music sounds like!

B. fill it mostly with music you like, but throw in some of her faves too—although you plan to mock her mercilessly when that sappy boy-band song that she loves so much comes on.

C. fill it with a lot of her favorite songs but throw in a few of your own too. If you introduce her to alternative stuff little by little, eventually you'll win her over to your side. For now you'll have to give her musical taste a chance.

D. fill it with all the music she likes. You know how much it must suck for her that her iPod is broken and you want her to be happy. You usually end up falling asleep on long bus trips anyway.

4. **You are volunteering at an animal shelter with a few elderly women from your neighborhood. There are only two jobs left for the day: bathing the full-grown German shepherd (who hates baths, by the way) and taking a few of the puppies into the playroom to help them socialize. You:**

A. choose the puppies, of course! They're sooo cute. Besides, you don't want to get your clothes all soaked when the shepherd shakes out his coat.

B. play with the puppies for a while, but eventually succumb to your guilt and go help with the German shepherd. With any luck, by the time you get in there, the big dog will have gotten most of his coat-shaking out of his system and you won't have to do too much.

C. suggest that you all do both jobs together. Even though it'll take a little longer, tackling the bath-hating shepherd might be easier if it's three against one. And then you can reward yourselves by playing with the adorable puppies before calling it a night.

D. roll up your sleeves and take the German shepherd on alone. It's a dirty job, but somebody's gotta do it, and it probably shouldn't be one of the elderly ladies, whose back problems make it hard to bend over the tub.

5. **The guy you like confesses to you that he sort of has a crush on your best friend and he wants you to tell her. You:**

A. tell him that your friend doesn't like him that way. You actually have no idea if that's true, but why ruin your own chance to hang with him? Since your BFF has never mentioned having feelings for him, you figure all's fair in love and war.

B. tell him that it's kind of lame to approach a girl through her best friend and that he should just get up the nerve to talk to her himself. You won't stand in their way, but come on! You'd have to be a saint to completely put aside your own feelings. Hopefully he'll be too chicken to go through with it on his own.

C. agree to tell your friend, but you tell her how you feel about him at the same time. You promise not to be mad if she likes him back, but you just want everything out in the open.

D. run and tell your friend right away and keep your feelings to yourself. Yeah, you did have a crush on him, but you guess he and your friend have more in common. If she does want to spend time with him, you'll just have to avoid hanging out with the two of them together for a while, until you get over him.

Give yourself 1 point for every time you answered *A*, 2 points for every *B*, 3 points for every *C*, and 4 points for every *D*.

—If you scored between 5 and 12, go to page 110.

—If you scored between 13 and 20, go to page 96.

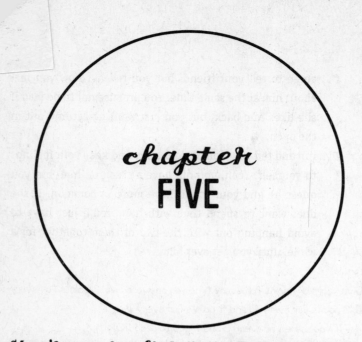

chapter
FIVE

You're a realist. You liked *The Notebook* as much as the next girl, but you realize that all that mushy stuff can wait. You're young and there are lots of adventures to be had first! Of your group of friends, you tend to be the grounded one who isn't ruled by her heart, so you can always be counted on to make a levelheaded decision. Just remember that eventually your heart will want to have its say too!

W ell, this just figures. Not only have you plowed into someone on your way to stardom, but the innocent bystander turns out to be none other than Jimmy Morehouse.

"I'm such a bonehead," you say, noticing his cool

checkerboard Skechers (which are splattered with paint) as you help him to his feet.

He rubs his head, which by now must be pounding. "It's okay. Really."

"Whoa! What a wipeout!" Lena cries. "We could hear the crash from inside the café."

"And, um, hate to tell you this," Jessie adds, "but we're not the only ones." She points down the hall, and there is Amy Choi standing in front of the Gap. She caught the whole incident on her video phone and is busy sending it out to her entire contact list.

"Great," you mutter. "This will be all over the school in five minutes." And the mention of time reminds you why you were in such a hurry in the first place. Oh no! To make it to the Photo Hut before Janice's deadline, you'll have to leave *now*. "Jimmy, I'm, like, really, really sorry," you tell him, noting how incredibly cute he is even with a golf ball–size knot forming on his head and dirt all over his T-shirt. "But I've gotta go."

"Go ahead," Lena urges you. "Carpe diem! We'll take care of the wounded here."

"What's that? Carpet D M?" you hear Jessie joke as you take off like a shot, heading for the Photo Hut. You hope Amy is getting some of *this* on tape, because you are giving an Olympics-worthy performance right now! First you leap over a stroller that some woman pushes into your path. Then, as you're running by the CVS pharmacy, a group of old ladies hobbles out with their walkers. You dodge among them like a pro. You run right past the huge half-off sale at Rampage, even though that jacket you've been wanting has finally been marked down. When you get to the escalators, you can see that the one going up is crowded and everyone on it is standing still. So you decide to run up the down escalator, which is clear except for Mark Bukowski and Kevin Minks, who are standing side by side. You crash right through them, your legs pumping so hard they feel like they're on fire. Lena would be proud. Maybe you should consider joining the track team this year.

"Hey, watch it!" Mark yells as you toss him aside.

"Are you b-b-blind?" Kevin calls after you, readjusting his World Series hat. "This is the d-down side, w-w-wacko!"

If you had any breath left in your body, you'd say you were sorry—especially for making Kevin stutter, which he only does now when he's mad or really nervous—but you don't, so you make a mental note to add them to the list of people you need to apologize to later.

Finally you arrive at the Photo Hut, which is all decked out in white sheets, with giant lights set up every few feet and what look like huge umbrellas. And there are models all over the place! You even recognize some of them from magazine ads. You could swear you just saw Mona—one of the brattiest girls in school—walk into a back room, but that can't be right. All the running must have your eyes playing tricks on you.

You clear the sweat off your face, and at last you spot Janice talking to some guy with a faux Mohawk. He's holding a clipboard and taking notes. This is probably the Steve you heard Janice talking to earlier. You tap Janice on the shoulder. "Hi, Ms. Iverson," you say cautiously. "I'm here, ready to be a model!"

"About time," Janice says without even looking at you. "Steve, let's get her measurements taken right away." She slowly turns toward you. "And then send her . . ." She trails off when she finally sees you. She clutches her chest with one well-manicured hand. "What happened to you?"

"What do you mean?" you say, still panting.

"I mean," Janice snaps, "you look like a wet dog."

Steve quickly pulls a compact mirror from his back pocket and holds it up to your face.

Oh my God. You look awful! Not only are you pouring sweat, causing your hair to droop like limp noodles, but your face has broken out into some serious acne. Maybe you should have stopped in a bathroom before you came in. You did just run hard enough to shed ten pounds on your way here—and it shows. But there's not much you can do about it at the moment.

"I can't use you now!" Janice stalks away furiously.

"But—" you start to protest, but Steve holds up a hand to stop you.

"Sorry, honey, but once she's like this, it's best to leave her alone for a while. Besides," he says, reaching out to touch your stringy hair, "she's right. You're a hot mess and we just don't have time to fix you right now. Better luck next time." He at least looks genuinely sorry for you as he backs away, already making calls to see if he can find your replacement.

In the words of Dr. Elliot Reid on that show *Scrubs,* frick on a stick! Looks like your modeling career is over before it even began. You notice that because of the mad dash you made, your legs now feel like jelly (or maybe that's how extreme disappointment feels as it settles into your body), so you find a bench outside the Orange Julius shop and sit down heavily, contemplating what part of the world you'll move to while you're trying to live down the shame. Iceland? Timbuktu? Canada? Living in any of them sounds better than facing your friends after this.

And just when you thought it couldn't get worse, your phone rings and suddenly Amy Choi is squealing into your ear.

"Eeeeeeee! Lizette just won a ticket!" she screams. You wait patiently for the second piece of news you're sure is coming. "And you know what else? There are only a few tickets left, but each one admits two people. So if you win, you can bring somebody. Isn't that awesome?"

Yeah, real awesome, you think after you hang up. Not only did you just get brutally rejected for a modeling job, but your odds of scoring a ticket to Shawna's party just got worse too. Maybe you should have just stayed in bed today. As you are thinking this, your Sidekick dings. You have a new text message from Jessie.

> Hey, supermodel! We R at JR
> with JM. News: JM is going to
> the party . . . with MW! But he
> keeps asking ??? about U. I
> think he likes you!

So while you are enduring the humiliation of your life at the Photo Hut, your friends are having a great time at Johnny Rockets with Jimmy Morehouse, and you're missing it—and he's Mona's date? Since when? On what planet is that even possible? Jimmy is way too nice to go anywhere with such a drama queen. But wait . . . what was that last part? Is it possible that he's asking lots of questions about you because he likes you? Could it be that the few times you managed to say anything to him actually made some sort of impression? Maybe the date with Mona is just some one-time thing but he really likes you. The very possibility makes you shoot up out of your seat—which is when you catch a glimpse of your reflection in the store window across the way. Ugh, gross! Yep, "hot mess" pretty much sums it up. You text Jessie back.

> Naaah . . . He prob'ly just
> wants to sue me for crashing
> into him + killing some of his
> brain cells. Call a lawyer!

A minute later she texts back.

```
LOL. :) I don't think so.
Comic-book geek + sprmodel
sitting in a tree . . .
```

You don't have the heart to tell her you won't be a model anytime soon, let alone a super one, so you flip your Sidekick closed and slip it into your pocket. "I think I'll just stay glued to this bench for the rest of the day," you say, moping.

"Yeah . . . I don't think that would be very productive," a deep voice says behind you.

You turn to see one of the most gorgeous guys ever. His short curly brown hair complements his deep hazel eyes perfectly, and when he smiles, his cheeks dimple just the tiniest bit. As he stands there with his thumbs hooked casually through the belt loops of his designer jeans, you realize that for some reason he's smiling at you! You clear your throat a few times before answering, hoping your voice doesn't come out as a nervous squeak.

"Oh yeah?" you answer. "What do you know about it?"

You didn't mean that to sound quite so defensive, but right now your pride is hurt and you didn't want any witnesses, let alone an insanely beautiful one.

"I know plenty, actually." He holds out his hand for you to shake. "I'm Elliott, one of the models on the Bebe

LaRue shoot you just ran away from. And I've worked with Janice for years. You wanna know how to get through to her?"

You nod, but half of you doesn't want to know.

He smiles sweetly. "You should ask for another chance!" When your eyes bug out, he chuckles softly. "I know, I know . . . sounds like suicide. But trust me, she responds to people who are more like her: really confident."

Hmmm . . . what Elliott says makes a lot of sense. But you aren't entirely sure you have "confident" in your repertoire at the moment.

"Anyway," Elliott continues, turning to leave, "just think about it. I've gotta get back to the shoot. I hope I see you there."

After he's gone, you think about what you really want to do now. On one hand, you feel like you should go back to the Photo Hut and fight for your right to model. On the other hand, you don't think that anything you say will sway Janice, so maybe you should just rejoin your friends and focus on finding Shawna. When did life at the mall get so complicated?

All right, so that didn't go exactly as planned. You made it to the Photo Hut in time for your big break, but it ended up being more of a big bust, thanks to some sudden monster acne. And to top it off, you skipped out on hanging with your übercrush, Jimmy, just to be rejected by Janice. Not that it matters, since Jimmy already has a date to the party—your archenemy, Mona. But it looks like all hope isn't lost. You've just met a walking billboard named Elliott who is not only sweet, but seemingly pretty smart. He's given you some decent advice, but only you can decide if you should take it. So get to the quiz and figure out what *you* would do next.

QUIZ TIME!

Circle your answers and tally up the points at the end.

1. **You're the star of the school play and the curtain is just about to go up. How do you feel?**

   A. Panicked! Your palms are sweaty, you can't seem to catch your breath, and you don't think you'll remember a single one of your lines. Is it too late to sneak out the back door?

   B. Scared silly but really excited too. Right now your stomach is full of butterflies, but you're praying they'll disappear as soon as you step out onto the stage. Anticipation is always the worst part.

   C. A little nervous, but jitters are to be expected on opening night. You know you'll probably make some mistakes, but that's part of the fun of live theater!

   D. Just fine. What's to be nervous about? You're completely prepared for this play and you're sure you'll do well. In fact, you might be the only actor on the stage whose hands aren't shaking!

2. **It's candy-selling time at school to raise money for the class trip, and whoever sells the most gets a trophy and no homework for a week! You each have to set a goal. You set yours:**

   A. pretty low. You are still reeling from the disaster that was your lemonade stand when you were little (two measly cups sold in three hours!). Your confidence has been shot ever since, so you'd rather set a goal that will be ridiculously easy to reach. You won't win the big prize, but if anybody asks whether you hit your goal, you can say yes— even though you did set the bar so low that only an ant could limbo underneath it.

   B. kind of low, but at least it's higher than the goal you set last year, which was basically "whatever I can sell to my mom." You have a feeling you'll be shot down, but you'll at least try to sell to your neighbors this time.

   C. fairly high. You aren't shooting for triple digits, like some of your classmates, but you've set a respectable goal. Even though you aren't positive you'll hit it, you're sure you can at least get pretty close and give yourself a decent shot at winning the trophy.

   D. off the charts. You believe so strongly in your ability to sell tons of candy that you ask your teacher for three extra order forms. Between your friendly, outgoing personality and a catalog full of chocolaty goodness, there's no way you'll lose. Besides, why aim low? You've got this competition in the bag.

3. **You attend your school's Fall Free-for-All—the first dance of the year—and they're playing your favorite song. You're itching to bust out some fancy footwork, but so far the dance floor is empty. What do you do?**

   A. Camp out by the snack table and try to look like you're way too busy scarfing down chips and punch to get out and dance. You're not exactly the get-the-party-started type and you're not sure whether your moves would make you a star or a laughingstock.

   B. Stand on the sidelines of the dance floor and nod along to the music. You don't want to play yourself by being the only person to get out there and dance—especially since you're not sure anybody would join you—but this song is too good to ignore completely.

   C. Wait till a few other brave souls get the dancing started, and then drag your friends out there so you can party the night away together. Now that the Free-for-All is finally in full swing, you're confident in your ability to dance with the best of 'em. (Hopefully everybody is having too much fun to bother critiquing your dance moves anyway.)

   D. You are the first one to hit the dance floor. You have absolutely no doubt that once you get out there, everybody else will follow your lead. And if they don't, who cares? At least you'll be having a good time.

4. **Your friends are up for some karaoke and they want you to choose the place. You pick:**

   A. the small karaoke machine in your room. You aren't sure you'll be able to belt out songs the way you want to in front of a roomful of strangers. What if your voice cracks? Uh-uh. At least if that happens, the stuffed animals on your bed will be the only witnesses.

   B. the coffee shop on the corner. It's a small, intimate setting, and usually the place is a ghost town on karaoke nights. (And hey, you aren't above faking a cold if you chicken out.)

   C. the popular karaoke place near the mall, where all the kids hang. Everybody there likes to pick songs that the whole room will sing along to. You won't feel unsure of yourself belting out a Katy Perry tune if all your friends are singing too.

   D. the nearby baseball stadium, where they have giant open mike nights for the whole town during the off-season. Why shouldn't everyone get to hear your fabulous musical stylings?

5. **The school is accepting candidates for student government and you want to be involved. You put your name in for:**

   A. secretary. It's a low-pressure position, you don't have to make any big decisions that your classmates might get on your case about, and you'll hardly be noticed at the meetings. Perfect!

B. treasurer. You'll be in charge of a student budget that puts your allowance to shame. And judging by how you did in your last math class, you're pretty sure you'll be able to deal with the big numbers.

C. vice president. Second-in-command is just where you belong. You don't have to worry about having the final say on things and possibly making the wrong decisions, but you're still high enough in the ranks to have a lot of important responsibilities. And if you drop the ball on anything, the prez will be right there to bail you out.

D. president. You know you have good ideas for the school and have no problem leading people. Yes, it's a job you've never done before and you aren't sure what kinds of things will be thrown your way. But you're confident that you can do anything you put your mind to, so you say bring it on!

Give yourself 1 point for every time you answered **A**, 2 points for every **B**, 3 points for every **C**, and 4 points for every **D**.

—If you scored between 5 and 12, go to page 96.

—If you scored between 13 and 20, go to page 123.

chapter SIX

Some people might call you nosey, but you prefer to think of yourself as curious. After all, don't the best journalists have to dig a little to get the scoop? And what is the nightly news if not one big gossipfest? But you could work on respecting people's privacy a little more. After all, you definitely wouldn't want anybody reading *your* diary!

Okay, it's not your proudest moment, but you totally eavesdrop on Mona and her mom. You can't help it! Finding out that Janice has a child is just too weird—especially since they don't even share the same last name.

Plus, you figure maybe you'll happen to overhear why Mona has it in for you.

You inch a little closer to the curtain, glad that you're barefoot at the moment.

"But, Mom, why do I even have to be here for fittings and everything? Everyone knows that I'm the star of the show, and everything fits me perfectly anyway."

Gag. She's worse than you thought.

"No one skips fittings, period," Janice tells Mona in that icy voice of hers.

"Moooom," Mona whines again. "I already told my date to Shawna's party to meet me here so we could figure out what he should wear. Since we're going together, I don't want him showing up in anything that'll make me look bad. So I'll just come back later, okay? It's not like anybody's going to start without the director's daughter."

But Janice is not having it. "Listen up, Mona. Just because you're my daughter does *not* mean you get any special favors around here, got it?"

"Ugh, whatever," Mona replies, and you can practically hear her eyes rolling. "What are you gonna do? Replace the star of the shoot?"

Janice laughs a little meanly. "Mona, you can easily be replaced. It only took me five minutes to find a model in the *mall,* of all places. So how hard do you think it would be for me to find another? Hm?"

Whoa. That shut her up.

"Besides," Janice continues, "I think you're too young to

be going on a date anyway. Even if it is with a nice boy like Jimmy Morehouse."

What? Did she just say "Jimmy Morehouse"? *Your* Jimmy Morehouse? Quiet, shy Jimmy is dating that monster? What did she do? Cast some sort of love spell on him? You're itching to know more, but it sounds like this conversation is almost over.

"Bottom line, you're not leaving. It's high time for you to grow up and be a professional!" Janice barks. You hear her stomp back to the set, leaving Mona speechless and no doubt pouting. Interesting. For the first time ever, you find yourself feeling a tiny bit sorry for Mona. Sure, she's no picnic, but then, neither is her mom.

You hear someone coming, so you scramble back to your seat in the small room where Steve left you. Steve walks in carrying a pair of gorgeous golden flats that match your outfit perfectly. He sighs with relief. "I finally found them in the accessories trunk. Try these on."

You slip into them as easily as Cinderella into her glass slipper. They're a perfect fit.

"Excellent!" Steve says, clapping his hands. "At least something went right today. We'll start doing test shots in about"—he checks his watch—"ten minutes. Don't. Go. Anywhere."

"*Sir, yes, sir!*" you cry, saluting him as if you are a soldier.

He shakes his head at you, clearly thinking, *Where did Janice find this weirdo?*

After he leaves, you pace around the tiny back room,

trying to process all this juicy new information you've learned: Janice has a kid. Mona may have inherited her rotten attitude from her model-scout mom. And quiet little Jimmy is going on a date with a nightmare. You're having a hard time wrapping your brain around that last one. You're utterly confused about how he could have accepted an invitation from Mona, of all people—especially since you thought for sure you and he had some sort of connection. But maybe that was just wishful thinking.

Before you have a chance to puzzle it out, Bryan strolls in, pushing his hair back with one hand. He's holding your phone and it is ringing off the hook. "Yours, I take it?" he says, holding it out to you.

"It is," you answer kind of self-consciously.

"That ringtone . . . Vampire Weekend, right?"

You smile as you nod and take the phone from him, your fingers grazing slightly. Bryan nods his approval. "Cool." Then he saunters out as slowly as he came in.

By the time you flip open your phone, just before the call would have gone to voice mail, your face is feeling all flushed. Bryan likes your music taste. Maybe he's even thought about going to a concert with you. . . . Wait! Weren't you just thinking about Jimmy? Ugh, it's all so confusing.

Anyway, you answer your phone, and—no surprise— it's Amy Choi. She is letting out a squeal so high-pitched that only dogs should be able to hear it. *"Eeeeeeee!* Lizette just won a ticket!" she shouts. "And you know what else?

There are only a few tickets left, but each one admits two people. So if you win, you can bring somebody. Isn't that awesome?"

That is pretty awesome, actually. Or at least, it would have been awesome back when you thought Jimmy could be your date. You really hope your friends are hot on Shawna's trail so that they both win and one of them can bring you. Or maybe if you get this fashion stuff over with quickly, you'll still have a shot at winning a ticket of your own. And since you obviously won't be hanging out with Jimmy anytime this century, you could bring one of your friends . . .

Just then Bryan comes skateboarding into the room and winks at you.

. . . or maybe you could bring someone else!

Well, at least now you know why Mona is such a witch sometimes. She gets it from her mother! But how she landed Jimmy is as big a mystery as where Shawna is hiding herself. Before you have time to feel the pain from that, though, another guy seems to be trying to catch your eye. You'll have to decide what to do about him, but right now, it's more important to figure out how to handle your archnemesis. After all, she could ruin everything for you! But do you have it in you to match her witchy behavior with your own? Take the quiz to find out.

QUIZ TIME!

Circle your answers and tally up the points at the end.

1. **You're trying out for the position of head camp counselor at Camp Chickasaw. It's been a tough competition, but now it's down to you and one other girl. Each of you must save a blow-up doll thrown into the lake. When you swim out, you reach her doll before your own. What do you do?**

    A. Pull out a pin you secretly stashed in your bathing suit and pop a hole in her doll in hopes that it'll deflate before she has a chance to reach it. Okay, so that's not entirely sportsmanlike, but you're here to win, not make friends.

    B. Purposely swim across her path, hoping that the splashing from your kicking feet will slow her down just the tiniest bit. There's nothing in the rules that says you have to swim in a straight line.

    C. Swim hard and fast for your doll, not even giving your competition a second look. If you win, you want to make sure it's fair and square.

    D. Push your competitor's doll closer to her. After all, if it were a real person, the point would be to save her life, right?

2. **You hear that the new girl in school has started an ugly rumor about you. You react by:**

    A. starting an even uglier rumor about her and posting it on your blog for the whole world to see, and saying snide

things under your breath whenever she walks by. Sometimes you have to fight fire with fire.

B. confronting her about it and yelling at her in front of the
entire cafeteria. You've got to put the new girl in her
place. Besides, she started it.

C. ignoring it. You and your friends know that the rumor
isn't true, and that's all that matters. Besides, the gossip-
mongers in your class have the attention span of goldfish.
This whole rumor business will blow over in no time and
they'll move on to talk about something else . . . you
hope.

D. switching schools. There isn't much point in taking a
stand now. Your rep here is o-v-e-r.

3. **You've been invited to a Halloween party and you want to go dressed
as Vanessa Hudgens's character in *High School Musical*. When you
get to the costume store, you see that there are only two of that
costume left. You:**

A. buy them both, just so no one else has any chance of wearing it. You want to be the only one who gets to show up as
Gabriella.

B. buy one and bury the other costume under a pile of clown
suits. Hopefully no one will find it there.

C. buy one and hope no one else comes in for the other one.
It would be cool to be one of a kind at the party, but
you aren't willing to do anything underhanded to make
sure your wish comes true—no matter how tempting the
thought may be.

𝐷. get on your cell phone and call your friends to tell them there's still one left in case one of them wants it. You'd love to be unique, but you and your friends are all *High School Musical* fans, so you can't deny them the chance to score such a hot costume.

4. **You are picked to help judge a talent show, and one of the singers is awful. We're talking *American Idol* open auditions awful. When it's time to give him your opinion, you are:**

𝒜. like Simon Cowell: brutally honest. Why sugarcoat it? What he did could barely be called singing. It was more like the sound of a howler monkey in pain. He shouldn't waste his time—or yours—pursuing a goal that he obviously won't reach. Instead, he should do the world a favor and stick to a silent hobby, like knitting or becoming a mime.

𝐵. like Kara DioGuardi: honest but tactful. You're still pretty hard on him, but you stop just short of making him cry. He shouldn't take your criticism personally anyway. He's gotta develop a thicker skin if he wants to make it in showbiz.

𝐶. like Randy Jackson: complimentary but full of constructive criticism. True, he wasn't the best singer you've ever heard in your life—okay, he was pretty close to being the worst—but at least he chose a great song to butcher, and maybe with some voice lessons he could sound a little less like fingernails on a chalkboard.

D. like Paula Abdul: nice to a fault. Sure, he sucked, but you don't want to kill his dream. So you tell him he has a "star quality," compliment him on what he's wearing, and avoid talking about his terrible singing altogether. Like you've always been told, if you don't have anything nice to say . . .

5. **You hear your younger sister telling your parents that she got an A on her last biology test, but you know for a fact that she got a big fat F. So naturally, you:**

A. threaten to tell on her unless she agrees to do all your chores for a month. What good is having the dirt on your sis if you don't use it to your advantage? She'd do the same thing if she were in your position, right?

B. make sure your sister knows that you know the truth and that you're keeping it to yourself . . . for now. You don't really plan to spill the beans; it's just fun to see her sweat. And it's also pretty cool to have something to dangle over her head, just in case.

C. tell your sister that you know she failed the test, and if she doesn't tell your parents the truth, you will. It's not that you want to see her get in trouble, but if your folks catch her in a lie, they'll just come down harder on both of you. Besides, it's not like your 'rents won't find out on Parent-Teacher Night anyway, and then your sister will really be in trouble.

D. clue your sister in that you know she failed the test. But you're no snitch. You don't plan to rat her out to your parents. But you also don't want to see her go down a road of academic loserdom and wind up getting left back. From now on you'll be tutoring her in biology so you can make sure her next test grade really is an A.

Give yourself 1 point for every time you answered *A*, 2 points for every *B*, 3 points for every *C*, and 4 points for every *D*.

—If you scored between 5 and 12, go to page 135.
—If you scored between 13 and 20, go to page 161.

chapter SEVEN

You have perfected the art of minding your own beeswax. Sure, it's tempting to dig up juicy details about others, but you are mature enough to realize that everyone deserves some privacy. And in a world where the stalkerazzi hide out in bushes to spy on celebs, and reality shows like *Keeping Up with the Kardashians* are the norm, your attitude is refreshing. Just make sure your tendency to mind your own business doesn't come off as not caring about other people. Your friends and family wouldn't mind if you showed a *little* interest in their lives.

It's clear that Janice and Mona have some issues to work out. And it would be pretty lame of you to eavesdrop on their conversation. So you head to the back room, where Steve is frantically looking for the gold flats that go with your outfit.

He is half buried in a huge trunk, full of accessories, on the floor. He flings garments all over the place as he goes. One satin scarf lands on your head, making you giggle.

"You think this is funny?" he demands. "If I don't find these shoes, Janice will kill me!"

If he were talking about anyone else, you'd tell him he was exaggerating. But with Janice . . . you think he might be right.

"Well, then I guess we'd better find them, huh?" you offer. "I'll check this other trunk." You get down on your knees, careful not to let your dress touch the floor. Then you start tossing stuff out of the trunk next to Steve's.

Steve looks up at you with his mouth wide open, clearly in shock. He absentmindedly strokes the mini Mohawk on his head. "You mean you're actually going to help me?"

"Duh," you answer. "Of course I am. I can fling clothes with the best of 'em, you know. You should see my room. And I'm always on the winning team in scavenger hunts. We'll find those shoes in no time."

"Wow," Steve says, looking dumbfounded. "I guess I'm just not used to anybody in this business being so . . . nice."

You stop flinging for a second. "You must mean Mona. I knew she was evil at school, but is she always like that?"

"Yes," a voice replies from the corner with no hesitation at all. "And you'd better get used to it if you want to work with her. She doesn't take kindly to sharing the spotlight."

"Yeah, that much I got," you say, seeing Bryan still sitting in the corner. "She can have the spotlight. Just gimme the clothes!" you joke.

He grunts—which you think is meant as a laugh—and goes back to playing his PSP.

"Ooh, you got the creature to stir," Steve says in mock surprise. "Impressive, considering the fact that we've been here since before the mall opened!"

"Jeez, so early?" You wince. "Why do you do this at all?"

Steve chuckles for the first time, finally loosening up a little. "You could say I'm in it for the clothes too."

You pull one of the size-6 blouses from the trunk in front of you and hold it against Steve's torso. "Hmmm . . . I don't know. I think these might be a little small for you."

He laughs again. "No, no, not wearing them—making them. I'm a designer. Or at least I will be someday."

"Cool!" you shout. "Then what are you doing here?"

"Well, I'm still in training. I have one more semester to finish at design school. Right now I'm interning at Bebe LaRue, which is how I ended up assisting Janice."

"Ooooh," you say. "No wonder you take so much abuse from her. Your degree depends on it, right?"

"That's it in a nutshell," Steve says sadly, checking his watch and reaching into the first trunk again.

You pull out a bundle of patent leather belts, and right beneath them, glimmering even in the darkness of the trunk, is a pair of perfect golden flats. "Eureka!" you cry. "I struck gold!" You hold them out to Steve, who hugs them to his chest.

"Oh, thank God! I was beginning to think I'd have to flee the country to escape the wrath of Janice. Thank you!"

You start picking up all the clothes lying on the floor and putting them back into the trunk. "No problem. Glad I could help prevent a homicide."

"Yes, well, if there's anything I can ever do for you, just name it."

"You could show me some of your designs. I'll bet you're really good."

Steve does another quick check of his watch. "Well, we do have about ten minutes before we have to get started. Hold on one second."

He runs out of the room, leaving you and Bryan in silence, save for the beeps coming from his PSP. One of you needs to break the ice, so you plunge in. "So, um, how do you know so much about Mona?" you ask tentatively.

"Aw, dude, Mona has a bad rep." He puts his game on pause and leans toward you in his chair. "You know that girl Alexa?"

You search your brain for a second, knowing you've heard the name before. "You mean the model who was supposed to be here today instead of me?"

Bryan nods seriously. "That's the one. Well, she and I got to be kind of good friends since I'm always meeting up with Steve at these things. She's pretty cool for a model." Before you have a chance to ask him what he means by that, he brushes his hair away from his face again and continues. "According to her, Mona actually told her to her face that her forehead was too big or something crazy like that, and that she should get out of modeling."

"Unreal!" you exclaim. "But, um, *was* it too big? Alexa's forehead, that is."

"No way," Bryan assures you. "Alexa is a ten, which is why Mona can't stand her. Besides, who decides how big a forehead should be, anyway?"

"*Vogue*, I think," you answer quickly. "Each issue comes with a little measuring tape so you can make sure you're not entering Frankenstein territory."

Bryan shakes his head, as if he wouldn't find that too hard to believe. "Chicks. Well, anyway, when that didn't work, Mona started pulling lame-o stunts like putting gum in Alexa's chair right before she was going to sit down, or just blocking her out of photos, you know? Typical mean-girl stuff. Straight outta the movies."

Ah yes, the old gum-in-the-chair bit. Mona pulled that particular brand of evil on you less than a week after you'd met. "I'm familiar with her work," you offer miserably.

Bryan nods again. "Well, then, you know that that routine gets old fast. So when this shoot came around, Alexa was gonna try to be tough and stick it out, but she decided that she had better things to do with her time than deal with a primo brat like Mona. Of course, she wasn't gonna tell dragon lady Janice that, so she had her agent make up some mumbo jumbo about her being double-booked, and she bounced."

"I don't believe it!" you say a little too loudly.

"Believe it," Bryan answers, leaning back in his chair and resuming his game.

You've learned a few things from that little interaction. One: Boys like to gossip just as much as, if not more than, girls do. Two: Bryan is pretty cute, though you wonder if Jessie would approve of him. (If Jessie equals fashion, then this guy equals anti-fashion. Either Jessie would be intrigued by his total lack of interest in what she feels is essential to life, or she would see him as a fun project.) And three: It's no accident that you got to be here today. You're filling the place left by someone who was driven away by Mona and her rotten attitude. Mona got rid of Alexa so that she wouldn't have to share her moment in the sun. No wonder she was so peeved when you showed up! Well, more than usual, anyway.

In Alexa's place, what would you have done? you ask yourself. At school you have no choice other than to deal with Her Royal Brattitude, but if you did have a choice, would you let Mona have the satisfaction of seeing you skip town or would you have the guts to stand up to her once and for all?

Before you can arrive at an answer, Steve rushes back into the room. He walks to the desk in the corner, unzips a case, displaying his sketches, and calls you over.

As you flip through them, you gasp. "Did I say I thought you'd be good? I was wrong. These are awesome!" Your eye lands on a cherry red jacket with dark square buttons and slanted pockets. "Especially this one. Love it, love it, love it!"

"Really?" Steve says happily. "Thanks. That's one of my favorites too." He pulls out a garment bag that was hanging on a hook and unzips it to reveal the red jacket and some incredible dresses. "I like to carry them around with me when I work on fashion shoots, just in case I should run into Dolce or Gabbana." He smiles.

"You're going to be bigger than both those guys put together," you assure Steve. "If you had been on *Project Runway*, you definitely would have won over Tim Gunn. Maybe even Nina Garcia!"

"Dare to dream," Steve says wistfully, zipping up the garment bag and putting away his portfolio. "For now, we've gotta get you back on the set. So put on the flats and I'll see you out there, honey. Come on, Bryan."

After they leave you slip into your shoes and are taking one final look in the mirror when you hear your phone ringing in your bag. It's Amy Choi and she is squealing like she just met all three Jonas brothers. *"Eeeeeeee!* Lizette just won a ticket!" she screams. "And you know what else? There are only a few tickets left, but each one admits two people. So if you win, you can bring someone. Isn't that awesome?"

You have to admit, it is pretty sweet. That means that if Lena and Jessie win tickets, they'll be able to bring you! Or even better, all three of you can win tickets so that Lena can bring Charlie (once you get her to admit that she might have a thing for him) and you can bring Jimmy (or possibly Bryan?), and you may even have someone in mind for Jessie. (You're not sure, but you think that one of the models on the set is the one in *Teen Vogue* Jessie was drooling over.) You really hope your friends are still in the running. It never hurts to have some backup plans.

But right now, you have a bigger fish to fry—namely, Mona Winston. She has already chased one model away. Are you next?

Isn't it funny? Sometimes when you try to mind your own business, information falls right into your lap! And it can come from the unlikeliest sources too. Steve revealed that he is not just some uptight Janice lackey, but a cool, talented designer. Amy told you all about Lizette's big win. And you got to talk to Steve's little brother. Who knew that skater-boy Bryan would give Amy Choi a run for her money in the gossip department? Good thing he did, though. At least now you know what to expect from Mona. The tricky part is figuring out what to expect from yourself. Is this where you strike a blow for models everywhere by standing up to moaning Mona? Or are you a little scared of her, making the stress of dealing with a bully so not worth the effort? Not sure? Take the quiz and find out.

QUIZ TIME!

Circle your answers and tally up the points at the end.

1. **You get your history test back, and your teacher took two points off for your answer about the Civil War. *No way!* you think. *My answer was dead-on!* So after class you:**

   A. march right up to your teacher and fight for your two points. You earned them! And if he refuses to budge, you'll go over his head and pay a visit to the principal. If that doesn't work, you may even try to find out how to call a press conference so the whole world will hear about this injustice!

   B. wait until after school, then approach your teacher and explain why you think you deserve those two points. He's an educated man; surely he'll see reason. And if not, you'll bug him about it every day until he does.

   C. write him an e-mail through the school's Web site, pleading your case. If he sees the light, great. But if he insists on sticking with his original opinion, you'll have to let it go. Why get mad when you can get even by knocking the next history test out of the park? No way will he be able to deduct a single point next time!

   D. sulk, but leave it at that. You think your teacher was dead wrong, but what's the use in fighting the grade? He probably won't change it anyway, and your friends will just think you're whining for nothing.

2. You've been standing in line for two long hours to be let into the advance screening of the summer's hottest new blockbuster movie. Rumor has it the whole cast will be in attendance! You already have your passes, but seating is limited, which means not everyone will be admitted. So you are understandably peeved when you catch three girls cutting the line. You:

A. speak up immediately, telling the latecomers to hit the road. There are enough people between you and the inside of the theater as it is. If they don't leave on their own, you have no problem with calling security over to give them the old heave-ho.

B. tap one of them on the shoulder and politely let her know that the line starts back there—*way* back there. Then point out the other people behind you who have been patiently waiting in line and are now glaring at the line-cutters.

C. say really loudly to your friends how much you *hate* it when people are totally *rude* and *cut the line*. You clear your throat a lot and stare daggers into the back of one line-cutter's head. Maybe they'll get the hint (or feel the waves of outrage you're sending their way) and leave on their own.

D. let it go. You don't want to make a scene, so you'll have to seethe in silence. But they'd better not have any more friends showing up later to join them in line.

3. You just met a really popular girl whose friendship would mean your being part of the in crowd. But she keeps calling you by a nickname that you absolutely hate. You:

A. ditch Little Miss Popular immediately. Anybody who would use that awful shortened version of your name within ten minutes of meeting you isn't worth your time. You'll find your own way into the in crowd . . . or you'll make an in crowd of your own.

B. correct her right away. That she's part of the cool kids' inner circle doesn't mean she gets to call you whatever she wants. Your name is fairly awesome and if she wants to be your friend, she should learn it now.

C. don't exactly correct her; you just find an excuse to say your own name a lot, and hope that she catches on. The name thing isn't a huge deal, but if you do end up being a permanent part of her clique, you'd hate to be stuck with a nickname that makes you puke.

D. let her use whatever name she wants! She can call you Donald Duck for all you care. The important thing is that you'll be hanging at the cool lunch table at long last—even if the other kids there don't know what your actual name is.

4. You're hired to babysit your neighbor's kids, who are six and seven years old. When nine o'clock rolls around, they want to stay up past their bedtime so they can watch the end of the Disney movie on TV. So you:

A. lay down the law and make them go to bed. There will be no mutiny on this ship! You're in charge, not them, so what you say goes. Really, they're lucky you've let them stay up this long.

B. call their parents so they can lay down the law. Sure, you could do it yourself, but having their mom and dad back you up is so much more effective. Plus, this way you get them to go to bed without looking like the bad guy.

C. agree to let them stay up an extra half hour, but the TV goes off. You'll spend that time reading them a bedtime story instead. You're betting they'll both be out like lights before you even get to the fifth page.

D. let them stay up. Nine o'clock isn't that late, and the movie is almost over anyway. Besides, you'd rather not deal with one of their infamous tantrums.

5. **You and a boy from school have plans to see the new Iron Man movie together. At the last minute, he cancels to go to a baseball game with the guys instead. You:**

A. tell him he can forget about going anywhere with you ever again. He clearly cares more about his friends than he does you. What a jerk!

B. let him have it! Your time is valuable too, and he shouldn't get into the habit of just blowing you off like that. If he wants you to keep hanging out with him, then he'd better shape up and start being more considerate.

C. tell him it's okay for him to cancel on the movie. You don't want to start a big fight right then. But a couple of days later, you tell him that bailing on you was kind of lame and you were really, really disappointed. Hopefully he'll understand and won't do it again.

D. act like you aren't mad at all (even though you totally are), but until you get over it, you do little passive-aggressive things to let him know you aren't happy with his behavior, like not returning his phone call that night and giving him the silent treatment during lunch the next day. That'll show him!

Give yourself 1 point for every time you answered **A**, 2 points for every **B**, 3 points for every **C**, and 4 points for every **D**.

—If you scored between 5 and 12, go to page 149.
—If you scored between 13 and 20, go to page 161.

chapter
EIGHT

From Chapter 4: You are the definition of "selfless." Not only do you put the needs of others before your own, but you are glad to do so. Clearly Mother Teresa is one of your role models. Just be careful that you aren't always sacrificing your own happiness for the sake of others. Sometimes you should get what you want too.

From Chapter 5: The good news is that you are not some egomaniac who always thinks she's the best one for the job. The bad news is that you don't ever seem to think you can do it. Have a little confidence. It's one thing to be humble; it's quite another to let insecurity prevent you from trying. Believe in yourself a bit more and you might find that you're a lot more capable than you think.

You're here with your friends — and Jimmy — at Johnny Rockets, but your mind has been a million miles away for several minutes now. "All right, campers," Lena finally says, clapping her hands and breaking the awkward silence, "all this sitting around and staring at the straw dispenser is fun, but we really need to get moving."

Thank God for Lena. Otherwise you might have just stayed in that booth, hoping a hole would open up in the floor so that you could crawl in. It's definitely time to snap out of it! Yes, it would have been great to be a model, but it wasn't in the cards. And as for Jimmy, you would have loved to be the Beyoncé to his Jay-Z, the Ashlee Simpson to his Pete Wentz, the Juliet to his Romeo — without all the crazy poison-drinking at the end — but that wasn't meant to be either. You doubt he would have been into you anyway if he likes someone like Mona. And the bottom line is he has a date to the party already. A *model* date, no less. How are you supposed to compete with that? True, you had a chance to be a model too, but that was just as a fill-in. Maybe Jimmy's artistic side is drawn to Gisele Bundchen look-alikes who learned to strike a pose before they even came out of the womb. What. Ever.

Besides, looking over at Jessie and seeing her freckled face light up when Lena mentions getting a move on, you realize she's just been biding her time for your sake. She wanted to give you and Jimmy a chance to talk, but inside she's been dying to continue the hunt for Shawna and the golden tickets. What a good friend.

So now it's time for you to be a good friend back and focus on scoring a pass to the party. You can cry in your room later.

After Jimmy settles the bill, the four of you head out into the hallway, which is still brimming with your class-mates, who are scattering in every direction. There're Megan Dunn and her cheerleading crew, heading into Bath & Body. Over by the water fountain are Anthony Tartelli and Dan Miner, lifting up potted plants, as if Shawna might actually be hiding under there. And walk-ing right by you is Charlie, with his color-coded map of the mall.

"Charlie!" Jessie calls out to him. "How's it going out there?"

Charlie walks over to your group, calmly ignoring the other kids running around like ants. "Well, I think I'm clos-ing in on her," Charlie confides in a low voice.

"What do you mean?" you ask.

He looks left, then right, clearly not wanting to share his info with the rest of the school. He motions for you to fol-low him to a nearby counter, where he lays his map flat and pulls out a bright red marker. The four of you crowd in around him and lean over the map.

"I've been tracking Shawna's movements," Charlie be-gins. "First she was sighted here at approximately ten fifteen." He marks a big red X over the Sephora store.

"Then she was here at ten thirty-five, where she gave a ticket to C. J. Flannigan."

"C.J. got a ticket?" Jessie interrupts. "What question did he have to answer?"

"He got a dare," Charlie said. "He had to eat ten jalapeño peppers in a row."

"Ouch!" you cry. "I hope I don't get something like that. I can't even handle buffalo wings."

"You would *so* be voted off the island on *Survivor,*" Jessie cracks. The two of you start giggling.

"Hey, focus, people, focus!" Lena says, snapping her fingers in your face. "We're running out of time, remember?"

You look at Charlie, who is waiting impatiently.

"Ahem . . . " You wipe the smile off your face, silently noting how quickly Lena tried to bring the attention back to Charlie. Aww . . . "Right. Sorry, Charlie. Go on."

Charlie leans back over the map. "As I was saying . . . she was here at ten thirty-five." He crosses out the GameStop. "Then, at eleven twelve . . ."

He goes on to cross out Things Remembered, CVS, Hallmark, and Payless ShoeSource. "As you can see," Charlie says, pointing with his long brown index finger to each of his neat red marks, "she's moving in a sort of circular pattern. She must have mall security helping her out, because she seems to be using the employee exits and hallways to get from store to store."

"You're brilliant!" Lena exclaims, eyeing the Shawna trail Charlie mapped out. You swear if she were a cartoon, her heart would be thumping right out of her shirt right now.

"So," Jimmy says, leaning closer to the map and sort of brushing against your arm as he does, "if she sticks to this pattern, she should show up somewhere in this area next." He points to the west end of the mall, which looks small on the map, but you know that it covers a lot of ground.

Jessie deflates. "How are we supposed to hit all those stores before Shawna runs out of tickets? That would be impossible!" She throws her arms up in frustration, and her bangles jangle like a drawerful of silver spoons.

"We split up," you suggest. "Everybody pick somewhere to go and we'll text each other if we find her."

"Good plan," Lena agrees. She looks down at the map. "What thinkest thou, m'lord?" she asks Charlie. "Whither should I go?"

Huh? Since when does Lena ask any guy's opinion? She's way too independent for that. Charlie's businesslike approach must be getting to her.

"Well," Charlie reasons, "I know Shawna loves going to the movies, so maybe start there?"

"I'm on it," Lena says, hoisting her pack onto her back. Before she goes, she turns to you and Jessie. "Farewell, friends. Parting is such sweet sorrow —"

"Yeah, yeah, yeah . . . Just step on it, Shakespeare!" Jessie interrupts, laughing as she spins Lena around and points her toward the movie theater.

As you watch your friend disappear down the hall, you shake your head, amused. "Freak."

Next up is Jessie. It's no secret that Jessie loves music, so before she says a word, you know exactly where she's headed. She takes a quick look at the map and slams her finger down on the square that says MUSIC MEGASTORE. "That's where I'll be. Wish me luck!" And off she goes, her blond ponytail bouncing as she jogs away.

"And what about you two?" Charlie asks, looking at you and Jimmy as if you are a team. *I wish!* you think. But maybe he'll stick with you and go wherever you decide to go. You cross your fingers—but no such luck.

"A-actually," Jimmy starts, checking his watch, "I really should be going. I'm late enough as it is, and Mona is probably going to kill me."

"Oh, right," you say quietly, the mention of him and another girl feeling like a tiny stab to your heart. "Yeah. Of course. Sure. No problem. Okay." *Would you stop it? You're rambling!* You take a breath. "Well, see ya later, Jimmy. Hope your head doesn't split open or anything."

"Um, thanks?" he says. *Ugh, was that a weird thing to say?* Yeah, that was probably weird. You should just stop talking now.

You smile and nod, waving as he walks away. *Sigh . . .* In your mind you see the happy balloon that was your hope of spending more time with Jimmy withering slowly into a shriveled rubber mess, as if someone let all the air out of it.

You guess it was dumb of you to think that you were the only one who noticed that Jimmy is pretty great. But you blame your intelligence-gathering crew (that means you, Lena and Jessie!) for not picking up on the single most important stat about him: he already has a date with Mona! You wish you had known that before you got your hopes up. Oh well. No use crying over spilled ketchup . . . not right now, anyway.

Charlie clears his throat, bringing you back to the here and now. You almost forgot he was still there.

"Huh? Oh, sorry. What were you saying?"

Charlie shakes his head slowly. "Got it bad for him, don't you?"

"What?" you object a little too loudly. "Who? Me? For Jimmy? Nuh-uh. I don't know what you're talking about." If Lena were here, she would say, "Methinks the lady doth protest too much." (Translation: Yes, you're totally gaga for Jimmy and you know exactly what Charlie's talking about.)

Charlie smirks, apparently not buying your denial at all. "Riiight. You're just staring a hole in his back because you're completely indifferent."

You open your mouth to object again, but realize it's useless.

"Okay, fine, you got me. Just do me a favor and don't tell that big mouth Amy Choi. And especially don't tell Jimmy!"

As if on cue, Amy pops out from behind you, her black

swishy hair swinging as if she's been running. "Did I hear my name?" she pants. "And don't tell Jimmy what?"

It's amazing! That girl is like a great white shark: She can sense a drop of gossip in the water from ten miles away. *Quick — make something up or Amy will make something up for you!*

"Uh . . . I was just saying don't tell Jimmy that everybody saw that video of us crashing into each other earlier, thanks to you. He'd be upset." Nice save.

"Oh, that," Amy says, disappointed, you guess, that you're talking about old news. She doesn't even have the decency to seem ashamed. "That was no big deal. And he wouldn't get mad, anyway. He's way too nice. Hard to believe he's going to the party with Mona."

"Yeah," you agree, struggling not to sound so miserable. "When did that even happen?"

Amy's eyes sparkle to life. *Goody!* you imagine her thinking. *I know something you don't know!* "You mean you didn't hear? I just found out today that Mona asked him to go, like, two weeks ago already, which is, like, forever!"

"But how did they meet?" you wonder out loud. "I mean, Jimmy never even spoke to her at school before summer vacation."

"Oh, they didn't meet at school. They met at, like, some modeling thing, you know? Because Jimmy's mom is, like, a makeup artist." Amy leans in toward you and Charlie, as if she's about to hand off some top secret information. Not that anything is top secret for Amy. "I hear that Mona sort of pushed Jimmy into being her date. And he just didn't want to hurt her feelings, so he said yes." With that, Amy straightens up again, adjusting her bangs. "But it's been so long now and he hasn't backed out. So maybe he really likes her," she says, shrugging. Just then Amy's phone beeps and she speed reads a text message. "Ooh! This could be good," she comments to herself. Then to you and Charlie she waves a quick good-bye. "Gotta go," Amy announces. "Duty calls!"

As Amy flounces away, Charlie—who looks even more businesslike after your run-in with the gossip fairy—turns to you and shakes the map in his hand. "Sorry about all that. But should we get back to finding Shawna? It might take your mind off things."

I might as well, you think, tears threatening to well up in your eyes. Even if he doesn't want to be, Jimmy is attached to Mona, which means your plan to spend more time with him is dead in the water. The only thing that could salvage this day is winning a ticket to Shawna's birthday party—even if you would have to see Jimmy there with Mona.

"Sure," you answer glumly. "Let me see that map."

The two of you study the color-coded squares together for a while before Charlie asks, "So? Where do you want to start?"

Aside from wanting to stalk Jimmy so you can confirm with your own two eyes that he actually likes Mona, you really aren't sure. But since you're not completely looney tunes (yet), you opt for the one place in the mall that always makes you feel better. You don't know if Shawna will be there, but right now you need a break.

Are you sure you aren't at an amusement park? Because today has been a total roller coaster so far. You gave up your chance at being a model—only to find out that your übercrush is going on a date with a model, who happens to be your sworn enemy, Mona. Rumor has it he was pushed into it, but that doesn't make you feel any better. And to top it off, all this drama has distracted you from looking for the birthday girl, Shawna. So maybe it's time to take Charlie's advice and get back to business. If you don't want to cry in front of everyone, though, it might be best for you to start somewhere that makes you feel safe and happy. Where would that be, exactly? Take the quiz and find out.

QUIZ TIME!

Circle your answers and tally up the points at the end.

1. **When you grow up, you want to be:**
   A. a rocket scientist. You would love pursuing the kind of career that only a handful of people in the world are smart enough to handle. You know that it would take lots of extra years of school, and you'd spend most of that time studying and reading, but for you, that's the fun part! Plus, you are crazy about science. Your friends may think

you're a super-geek, but you know there's nothing wrong with using your brain to the max.

B. an English teacher. You're always correcting everyone's grammar anyway, so this seems like a good fit. Besides, from Shakespeare to Stephenie Meyer, you've read it all, and nothing would suit you better than to be in a class-room day after day, sharing your love of books with your students.

C. a Web site designer. Some serious computer skills are nec-essary for this gig, but once you have those down pat, you can be as creative as you want. And your Web sites would never be boring, since you'd know how to jazz 'em up with animation, streaming video, interactive links, music, and whatever colors or crazy fonts you could think of!

D. an art photographer. What could be better than traveling the world in search of that perfect shot, and possibly hav-ing your work hang in a gallery one day? Your family might think you're cuckoo because you have no steady address (and no steady paycheck), but hey, that's the life of an artist!

2. **Your ideal holiday present would be:**

A. the deluxe, oh-my-God-these-questions-are-so-hard edi-tion of Trivial Pursuit. You prefer presents that will give your brain a real workout (although it's already pretty buff).

B. the complete collection of the Sisterhood of the Traveling Pants books. Fun, friendship, and love all wrapped up with some great writing and smart female characters? Yes, please!

C. the computer game that lets you design your own roller coaster. Figuring out how to design a ride that is fast and safe is actually a lot more complicated than people think, but you would love getting to decide how the ride would look and what kind of death-defying turns and loops you could throw in there.

D. an easel and canvas with a full set of acrylic paints—the ideal companions for an *artiste* (that's "ar-teest") such as yourself. The only thing better than going to a museum to see priceless works of art is to put some paint on a canvas and create one of your own! It's the perfect way to let your imagination run wild.

3. **The walls of your room are:**

A. plain white, with a map of the world on one and a framed photograph of Albert Einstein on another. And don't forget the Socrates quotes above your bed. Oh, and all your academic achievement awards and science fair plaques . . .

B. tan, with a simple corkboard where you tack up your best and worst test scores. The good scores make you feel smart, and the not-so-great scores motivate you to work harder.

C. blue, with a few framed photos of your friends and family. The blue is a soothing, relaxing color that makes you think of the ocean. And it's always nice to see your loved ones' faces smiling back at you.

D. bright purple, with pictures of all your favorite things covering almost every inch of space. Near your bed are the scrapbook-type collages you made of your friends, with funny sayings underneath, and your mom lets you keep a string of colorful twinkle lights up all year long because you think they look festive.

4. **Your history teacher gives you an assignment to write about a woman who inspires you. You choose:**

A. Marie Curie. She was a physicist and a chemist, and she was the first person to win a second Nobel Prize and the first female professor at the University of Paris. Basically, she kicked scientific butt! If you accomplish half as much as she did, you'll be happy.

B. Hillary Clinton. She's a strong, educated woman who came from Wellesley and Yale Law School and ended up almost making it to the White House! She seems to care about people, and even if she hadn't become the secretary of state, she still would have been an amazing lawyer.

C. Emma Watson—one of your favorite actresses. Of course she played a know-it-all on-screen when she starred as Hermione in all the Harry Potter movies, but she's a smarty-pants in real life too! She was accepted into Yale, Cambridge, and Brown. Gotta love a girl with brains and talent.

D. Maya Angelou. She's a writer, dancer, artist, actress, and all-around creative soul. There is nothing artistic that this woman can't do. She's even won a few Grammys! That's your kind of role model.

5. **You and your parents are strolling along the boardwalk on the beach when you see a palm-reading table. Do you stop to get your palm read?**

   A. What for? Everybody knows there's no scientific proof to show that any of that stuff is real. You haven't seen any hard evidence that anything a palm-reader says is true, so you wouldn't waste your time—or your parents' money—on that.

   B. You probably won't have your palm read. You don't buy into any of that, really. But you'll stop to watch someone else have theirs read, just for fun.

   C. Why not? You aren't sure you believe that the palm-reader can see your future, but hey, you never know. If you're about to run into that adorable guy from your math class, you wouldn't mind a heads-up!

   D. Of course! You're open to all the mysteries of the universe. And the palm-reader's shimmering silk scarves and amber rings speak to your creative side. Before she even asks if you want a reading, you're sitting in the chair across from her with your palm in her face.

Give yourself 1 point for every time you answered *A*, 2 points for every *B*, 3 points for every *C*, and 4 points for every *D*.
   —If you scored between 5 and 12, go to page 184.
   —If you scored between 13 and 20, go to page 173.

chapter
NINE

You're no shrinking violet. When it comes to getting what you want, you aren't shy at all. That can be a good trait in some situations. You should never be afraid to demand the things you deserve. The problem is you think you deserve everything and rarely consider what anybody else wants. Sometimes seeing someone else happy can make you feel even better than getting your own way does.

"All right, campers," Lena says, clapping her hands and breaking the awkward silence, "all this sitting around and staring at the straw dispenser is fun, but we really need to get moving."

You shoot Lena a look. Is she nuts? If you go now, Jimmy

will leave to meet Mona. Not how you want this to play out at all. True, he's taking Mona to the party, but that doesn't necessarily mean that he really likes her. You're sure that if he just spent a little time with you, he'd see that you two would have way more fun together. But that means you can't go splitting up right now. What you need is a plan.

You're still trying to come up with one as Jimmy settles the bill and you all file out of Johnny Rockets. The halls are teeming with your classmates, who are running around the mall, frantically looking for Shawna. Just seeing all of them clearly lights a fire under Jessie, who is bouncing up and down where she stands. "Let's go, let's go, let's go!" she shouts.

And just when all hope seems lost, you spot the most beautiful thing in the mall against the far wall. With its drab brown curtain and faded lettering, you almost missed it. But now it seems to glow with an angelic light, and you can almost hear the trumpets in the background, hailing your next great idea. The photo booth! It's perfect. Lots of people + tiny space = you getting much closer to Jimmy. Being in there with your friends is always fun, but posing for shots with Jimmy would probably be superromantic. And this could be your last chance before he runs off to meet (gag) Mona. So it's now or never.

"Wait!" you cry, tugging the back of Jessie's T-shirt, not giving her a chance to get away. "Before we go, we should really pile into the photo booth over there and take a few pictures. You know, to remember this day by."

Lena, Jessie, and Jimmy don't seem too into this idea. They all start shifting around uncomfortably, and Jimmy starts rubbing his head again.

"Now?" Jessie asks incredulously. "Have you gone all head-shaving Britney on me or something? There are only a handful of tickets left."

"And we're seriously running out of time," Lena adds reasonably.

"Plus, I'm already pretty late as it is to meet my, um . . . you know. She's probably going to kill me."

These are all compelling reasons not to get into the photo booth, but you still want what you want. It's time to pull the guilt-trip card.

"Oh," you say in your saddest voice, looking down at your shoes. "Okay . . . I just thought that since I missed out on a chance to be a model today, it might make me feel better to at least take some pictures with my friends. But that's all right. I understand." You shrug and wipe an imaginary tear from your eye. Oh, you're good.

The three of them look at one another, and Lena lets out a sigh. "Okay. Maybe just a few quick pictures. Get thee to a photo booth, and quickly too!"

You immediately brighten up. "Yay!" You grab Jimmy's hand and pull him toward the booth. "Come on!"

Inside, it's a lot smaller than you remembered, with just one tiny bench that barely seats two people and a sliver of standing room behind it. Right away you decide that you and Jimmy need to be on the bench so that you have an excuse to sit close to him. The blood circulation to Jessie's and Lena's legs will probably be cut off as they to squish in behind you, but they're good friends. You're sure they don't mind taking one for the team. You look back at them, certain that they understand the romance of this moment and will be beaming back at you. Instead, they just look antsy and a little bit mad. And Jimmy keeps checking his watch and biting his lip.

Though the booth itself is old, they have upgraded the photo machine so that it takes digital pictures and you have the option of viewing them first before you print them. You slip in your three dollars and press the Start button. Before you even have a chance to sit back, the flash goes off, blinding you.

"Hey! I wasn't ready yet!" you cry.

Flash!

"What's wrong with this thing?" you say angrily. "I didn't even get to—"

Flash!

"Stop that!" you say, as if there's a person back there taking the snapshots. "Everybody get ready—"

Flash!

You know that the machine takes only four pics at a time, so you've already blown this round. You press View, and when the pics show up on the screen, all your friends start laughing hysterically. In the first one, your forehead is filling up almost the entire frame. In the second one, your mouth is wide open and your eyes are unfocused. Jimmy is

113

blinking, so it kind of looks like he was asleep, and Lena and Jessie are behind you, trying to hold in a laugh. The next one is even worse. You're shaking a fist at the camera, your eyebrows knitted in anger. In the last one, you're not even facing the camera. It's a great shot of the back of your head and everyone looking at you as if you're a mental patient.

"Great looks," Jessie says, doubling over with laughter — well, as much as she can double over in this cramped booth. "Kind of like those Mischa Barton mug shots."

"You definitely missed your calling," adds Lena. "I especially like the fist-of-fury shot." She holds up her fist and scrunches up her face.

Okay, okay, it *was* pretty funny. You start laughing too, glad that something loosened everybody up, even if it had to be your utter embarrassment.

"How 'bout we try that again?" Jimmy resets the camera and pauses with his finger over the Start button. "Okay, everybody get ready now."

Jessie and Lena link arms and lean in. You take the opportunity to link your arm with Jimmy's and scoot a little closer. His face turns bright red and he clears his throat nervously. "Here we go," he announces, his voice cracking slightly.

He pushes the button and sits back quickly. Two seconds later, you're all blinded by the flash.

"Funny face now!" you call out. You stick your tongue

out to the side and cross your eyes. Jimmy hooks two fingers in his mouth and pulls the corners as far as they'll go. Jessie sucks in her cheeks and makes her eyes big and round—her famous fish face. And Lena imitates your fist-of-fury shot again.

Flash!

You all crack up. "Now pretend there's an earthquake!" Jessie yells.

You immediately swing one leg over Jimmy's lap and pretend you're being tossed around the booth. Everybody flails their arms and screams, "Whooooa!"

Flash!

Now you're laughing so hard your face hurts. And when you look at Jimmy, he's staring right back at you, his messy brown hair hanging over his gorgeous green eyes. He is so Milo Ventimiglia in *Heroes,* you can't stand it. And for a moment it's like you two are the only ones in the whole mall. You're mesmerized.

Flash!

"I have to hand it to you—that was fun," Jessie admits, breaking you out of your trance.

"Definitely," Lena says. "Now just press Print and let's get out of here. My legs are falling asleep!"

You reluctantly move away from Jimmy so you can pull back the brown curtain and squeeze out of the booth. Jimmy and your friends are right behind you. You check the slot where the photos come out, and there is already a strip of pictures there. "Wow! That was fast," you tell everyone. "Usually that takes a couple of minutes at least."

But when you pull the strip toward you, you see that they aren't pictures of you and your friends at all. They're pictures of Shawna! "Huh? What are these doing here?"

"Hey, there's writing on the back," Jimmy points out.

You turn the strip over in a hurry and see Shawna's neat handwriting. You read it out loud.

> "Whoever found this strip,
> you just missed me!
> Study the pictures for clues and you
> just might get your golden ticket!"

The four of you crowd around the photos, your heads almost touching. In each shot, Shawna is wearing dark glasses and a trench coat, so you can't see what she has on underneath. But she has different accessories each time. Jessie zooms in on the iPod sticking out of one pocket in the first shot. "Check out the nano," she says. "Maybe that means she likes music. I'll go to the Music Megastore and see if she's there." Before you even have a chance to argue, Jessie is jogging away, her ponytail bouncing happily behind her.

Lena, meanwhile, studies the second frame. "Hey, is that a tub of popcorn next to her on the bench? You can only get those at the movie theater. I'm going to go check it out!"

And Lena is gone in a flash, leaving you and Jimmy standing together. Finally you're alone! You're sure that after the great time you had in the photo booth, he's forgotten all about his meeting with Mona and wants to spend the rest of the summer with you—or at least, the rest of the afternoon.

"So where should we go?" you ask, smiling up at him.

But he just hands you the strip of photos and looks sadly at his watch. "I'm so sorry," he tells you, "but I should really go. I'm beyond late."

He heads down the hallway, yelling, "Good luck!" over his shoulder. You stand there for a second, sadly watching his back as he sprints away. Did you just imagine the moment you shared in the photo booth? Was his arm touching yours only in your mind? You're crushed. You were so sure your plan would work you even risked making your friends mad at you—all for nothing.

As you stand there, the photos you and your friends just took finally drop into the slot.

Only when Jimmy is completely gone from view do you bother to glance down at them. They came out great. But seeing how happy Jimmy looked while sitting next to you makes tears well up in your eyes. So you quickly shove the strip into your back pocket and focus on Shawna's clues.

In one of the remaining two photos, Shawna is wearing a beret and holding a paintbrush. In the other, she has a bookmark sticking out of her pocket. Hmmm . . . You have a couple of ideas about where those clues lead. The question is, which clue do you choose?

It seems that selfishly putting your own needs ahead of your friends' doesn't necessarily get you what you want. Sure, you had a great time in the photo booth, but in the end, Jimmy still left to find Mona and you got your heart broken again. And Lena and Jessie took off mighty quickly too. Yes, they wanted to go find Shawna, but could it be that they were still a tiny bit peeved by the way you manipulated them to get your way, and they needed a little break from you? Very possibly. Perhaps it's time to rededicate yourself to the mission and prove to your friends that you're on their team. But which clue are you leaning toward? The next quiz should clear it up for you.

QUIZ TIME!

Circle your answers and tally up the points at the end.

1. When you grow up, you want to be:
   A. a rocket scientist. You would love pursuing the kind of career that only a handful of people in the world are smart enough to handle. You know that it would take lots of extra years of school, and you'd spend most of that time studying and reading, but for you, that's the fun part! Plus, you are crazy about science. Your friends may think

you're a super-geek, but you know there's nothing wrong with using your brain to the max.

B. an English teacher. You're always correcting everyone's grammar anyway, so this seems like a good fit. Besides, from Shakespeare to Stephanie Meyer, you've read it all, and nothing would suit you better than to be in a classroom day after day, sharing your love of books with your students.

C. a Web designer. Some serious computer skills are necessary for this gig, but once you have those down pat, you can be as creative as you want. And your Web sites would never be boring, since you'd know how to jazz 'em up with animation, streaming video, interactive links, music, and whatever colors or crazy fonts you could think of!

D. an art photographer. What could be better than traveling the world in search of that perfect shot, and possibly having your work hang in a gallery one day? Your family might think you're cuckoo because you have no steady address (and no steady paycheck), but hey, that's the life of an artist!

2. **Your ideal holiday present would be:**

A. the deluxe, oh-my-God-these-questions-are-so-hard edition of Trivial Pursuit. You prefer presents that will give your brain a real workout (although it's already pretty buff).

B. the complete collection of the Sisterhood of the Traveling Pants books. Fun, friendship, and love all wrapped up with some great writing and smart female characters? Yes, please!

C. the computer game that lets you design your own roller coaster. Figuring out how to design a ride that is fast and safe is actually a lot more complicated than people think, but you would love getting to decide how the ride would look and what kind of death-defying turns and loops you could throw in there.

D. an easel and canvas with a full set of acrylic paints—the ideal companions for an *artiste* (that's "ar-teest") such as yourself. The only thing better than going to a museum to see priceless works of art is to put some paint on a canvas and create one of your own! It's the perfect way to let your imagination run wild.

3. **The walls of your room are:**

A. plain white, with a map of the world on one and a framed photograph of Albert Einstein on another. And don't forget the Socrates quotes above your bed. Oh, and all your academic achievement awards and science fair plaques . . .

B. tan, with a simple corkboard where you tack up your best and worst test scores. The good scores make you feel smart, and the not-so-great scores motivate you to work harder.

C. blue, with a few framed photos of your friends and family. The blue is a soothing, relaxing color that makes you think of the ocean. And it's always nice to see your loved ones' faces smiling back at you.

D. bright purple, with pictures of all your favorite things covering almost every inch. Near your bed are the scrapbook-type collages you made of your friends, with funny sayings underneath, and your mom lets you keep a string of colorful twinkle lights up all year long because you think they look festive.

4. **Your history teacher gives you an assignment to write about a woman who inspires you. You choose:**

A. Marie Curie. She was a physicist and a chemist, and she was the first person to win a second Nobel Prize and the first female professor at the University of Paris. Basically, she kicked scientific butt! If you accomplish half as much as she did, you'll be happy.

B. Hillary Clinton. She's a strong, educated woman who came from Wellesley and Yale Law School and ended up almost making it to the White House! She seems to care about people, and even if she hadn't become the secretary of state, she still would have been an amazing lawyer.

C. Emma Watson—one of your favorite actresses. Of course she played a know-it-all on-screen when she starred as Hermione in all the Harry Potter movies, but she's a smartypants in real life too! She was accepted into Yale, Cambridge, and Brown. Gotta love a girl with brains and talent.

D. Maya Angelou. She's a writer, dancer, artist, actress, and all-around creative soul. There is nothing creative that this woman can't do. She's even won a few Grammys! That's your kind of role model.

5. **You and your parents are strolling along the boardwalk on the beach when you see a palm-reading table. Do you stop to get your palm read?**

   A. What for? Everybody knows there's no scientific proof to show that any of that stuff is real. You haven't seen any hard evidence that anything a palm-reader says is true, so you wouldn't waste your time—or your parents' money—on that.

   B. You probably won't have your palm read. You don't buy into any of that, really. But you'll stop to watch someone else have theirs read, just for fun.

   C. Why not? You aren't sure you believe that the palm-reader can see your future, but hey, you never know. If you're about to run into that adorable guy from your math class, you wouldn't mind a heads-up!

   D. Of course! You're open to all the mysteries of the universe. And the palm-reader's shimmering silk scarves and amber rings speak to your creative side. Before she even asks if you want a reading, you're sitting in the chair across from her with your palm in her face.

Give yourself 1 point for every time you answered *A*, 2 points for every *B*, 3 points for every *C*, and 4 points for every *D*.

—If you scored between 5 and 12, go to page 184.

—If you scored between 13 and 20, go to page 173.

chapter TEN

Finally, a girl who really believes in herself! You aren't afraid to put yourself out there, because you have faith in your abilities and know what you have to offer. Your confidence makes you a born leader. Just be sure you're realistic about your limits. Even Oprah has her off days.

After you sit on the bench awhile longer, licking your wounds, you decide that Elliott has a point. You can't mope on the bench all day. And the truth is you know you could do a great job if Janice would just give you a chance. Besides, you also know that Elliott is eagerly waiting to see what you'll do, and no way do you want to take the wimpy road in front of him.

"All right," you say to yourself. "I'm going back in." You stand up and catch your gross reflection again. "But not like this!" You head straight for the bathroom to clean yourself up a little. You pull your hair back with a headband you find at the bottom of your bag, splash some water on your face, and dab on a little lip gloss. That's better! Checking yourself out in the mirror, you think, *Not bad*. But you're still a little ashamed that you let Janice drive you away like that. Who is she to tell you that you aren't good enough? She clearly had no idea that she was in the presence of the world's best babysitter, the girls' soccer team MVP, and the undefeated Cranium champ. (Jessie and Lena can vouch for that last one.) Bottom line, you can do anything you set your mind to—and now it's time to prove it.

Before you have a chance to chicken out, you march straight back to the Photo Hut. Models are still milling around everywhere. Steve is huddled in a corner, nervously chewing on the end of a pen and making phone call after phone call, while Janice is pacing back and forth like a hungry lion. And wait a minute . . . is that Mona—the most obnoxious girl in school—getting her hair teased in the back? Ugh. Guess your eyes weren't playing tricks on you earlier after all. What is *she* doing here? You've heard from Amy that Mona has done some modeling. You just never believed her. But there Mona is in full spoiled-brat mode. She loves nothing better than to watch other people fail, so it would really suck to get rejected (again) in front of her, especially now that you know she snagged a date with Jimmy, a fact you still can't quite believe. Um, are you sure about this? It's not too late to turn back, you know. Jessie and Lena would understand if you just walked away right now and drowned your sorrows with a vanilla milk shake.

No way, you tell the voice in your head. You deserve this. You'd be good at this. Sure, you're shaking like a leaf inside, but why let that — and a few silly pimples — stop you? Just then you spot Elliott, who is smiling a big excited grin and giving you two thumbs up.

How sweet is he? You find yourself wondering how old he is. He doesn't look older than fourteen. Jessie would totally approve of him for you — if only as another possible crush.

"Here goes nothing," you tell yourself.

You square your shoulders, walk right up behind Janice, and tap her on the shoulder. She whirls around, takes one look at you, and says, "You again? Didn't I dismiss you already?"

"Yes," you answer quickly. "But you were wrong."

Over Janice's shoulder you see Steve gasp and cover his mouth with one hand. Even his mini Mohawk is quivering.

"Excuse me?" Janice says in an ice-cold voice, narrowing her eyes at you.

"You were wrong," you repeat without hesitating. "I'd be awesome in this photo shoot. *Top Model* happens to be my favorite show and I know all the tricks. I even know how to smile with my eyes. . . ." You demonstrate one of Tyra's patented moves, looking off to the side and squinting your eyes just a little. "You'd be crazy not to hire me."

Janice leans back and puts her fists on her hips. Well, at least she hasn't bitten your head off yet. That would really put a crimp in your day.

"You know what?" she begins, and you're fairly sure you're about to be told off in stunning fashion. "I like your spunk."

What's that? Did she just say she likes you?

"It took a lot of guts to come back here." Janice steps toward you, taking your chin in her hand. And just when you think she's going to be affectionate and sweet . . .

She roughly turns your head from side to side. "But look at all this acne! I'm sorry, but what am I supposed to do with this? *Sheila!* Get over here," she barks.

A plump older woman comes toddling out from the back, carrying what looks like a tackle box. "You rang?"

"Look at this one," Janice orders. "Is there something you can do to cover up her skin in the next, say, ten minutes?"

Sheila studies your face, which Janice is still turning from side to side so hard you're sure you'll get whiplash. "I'm good, but I'm no miracle worker," Sheila admits. "There just isn't enough time to fix this for today's shoot."

Janice looks back at you and shrugs. "Sorry, kid. Better luck next time." She starts to walk away without even looking back at you. Steve winces at you and mouths, *Sorry.*

Ouch. You're zero for two. You're proud of yourself for giving it another shot, but how are you going to face your friends? They were more excited about your modeling than you were. How are you going to break it to them that not only did you *not* score any free clothes, but you didn't even step foot on the set? And you don't even want to think about Elliott, who is probably watching the humiliation unfold as you speak. What would he do in this situation?

You are tempted to mope your way down the hall again when suddenly you hear Steve's phone ring with a Rihanna song. He snaps it up quickly and you hear him say, "Oh God. Please tell me you're kidding. Janice is *not* going to like this."

Janice, only a few paces away, demands to know what's going on now. Steve tells the person on the phone to hold on, then seems to brace himself to deliver the bad news. "Natasha, the model I called you about earlier who fell off her stilettos? Well, they're releasing her from the hospital."

"So? What's the problem?"

"She's in a full leg cast. She definitely won't be able to be in the commercial today." Steve takes one step back, in case Janice is about to start breathing fire.

"Great!" Janice yells. "First Alexa, now Natasha? I suppose I can have Mona wear all the necessary outfits for this photo shoot. But who am I supposed to get to replace Natasha in the commercial! The SmoothSkin reps are going to be here this afternoon. Thanks to the deal Bebe worked out with them, they definitely want the commercial shot in this godforsaken mall using a model I selected. I really don't have time to hold auditions, and I need somebody with a fresh face now!"

Bingo! That's your cue!

You step right into Janice's line of vision and say, *"Ahem!"* as loudly as you possibly can. When she looks your way, you smile your biggest, cheesiest smile. "One fresh face, at your service."

Before Janice can even think about dismissing you again, Steve says into her ear — just loud enough for you to hear him — that you would be the perfect girl to illustrate both the "before" and "after" parts of the face-wash commercial. "I mean, who better to show how well the product works than a girl who really needs it?"

"And how are we supposed to film the 'after' segment, genius?" Janice snaps. "Photoshopping isn't in the budget."

Steve strokes his Mohawk thoughtfully as he studies your face. "Well . . . we could always tape the last part of the commercial next week, after she's had a chance to actually use the product. By then the acne should be all cleared up."

Janice can't argue with that logic. She takes a deep breath and says, "All right. You're in. But don't screw it up! And by next week, I don't want to see a single zit on that face, understood?"

You nod quickly, afraid to say any more.

"Good. Steve, you fill her in on what she has to do and

inform her mother about the change in plans. I've got to go set up this shot with one less girl." She stalks away, barking orders as she goes.

Yes! This worked out even better than you hoped! Not that you want to be known as that girl with the bad skin, but still . . . a commercial! Wow! Jessie and Lena are never gonna believe this. You just hope you can pull it off.

You're just about to send them a text message update when someone pats your back gently.

"Congratulations!" Elliott says happily as you spin around to face him. "That was awesome! You're going to do great."

Once you get over your unexpected joy at having this gorgeous guy showing you any sign of affection, you're nervous all over again. You've never done any professional acting before. Can you really pull off a commercial? Guess you're about to find out.

Good for you! You showed the world—and more important, yourself—that you have a lot of confidence, which people like Janice respect. You didn't let her give you "no" for an answer and ended up scoring a part in a commercial! You also managed to befriend a totally hot male model, who has definitely taken your mind off Jimmy for the time being. Not bad for a day's work! With the roll you're on, you wouldn't be surprised if

Shawna showed up at the commercial set. Still, you've talked a good game, but can you really deliver? Or will the pressure be too much? Take the quiz and find out if your nerves will get the best of you.

QUIZ TIME!

Circle your answers and tally up the points at the end.

1. **You're in the middle of an oral report that you had to memorize for Spanish class and you forget the second half of your speech. What do you do?**

    A. Come to a complete halt and run out of the classroom. You can barely remember how to speak English right now, let alone Spanish. True, running out mid-*examen* won't earn you any grade points with the teacher (or cool points with your friends), but it beats dealing with this pressure!

    B. Struggle through it, blurting out whatever random lines of the speech you can remember. Unfortunately, you're remembering them all out of order and no one knows what you're saying. Finally you give up and beg the teacher to let you try again tomorrow.

    C. Wing it. You start making things up right on the spot. You're making absolutely no sense and you're pretty sure you just said something like "Cats eat green eggs at midnight," but at least you're still talking. And maybe your teacher will be so distracted by how well you roll your *r*'s that she won't notice that your speech just went from Spanish to gibberish.

    D. Stop, take a deep breath, and get your bearings. You know you can nail this speech if you just stay calm. Once you get past the nerves, the rest of the words will come flooding back to you. And if not, you'll just talk about the topic in your own words. It might not be as good as the speech, but the point is to show how well you can speak Spanish.

2. **If you could be on any game show, it would be**:

   A. *Deal or No Deal.* You have plenty of time to think and ask your family and friends for help—and talk smack to the banker. And all you have to do is pick numbers, so even if you were nervous, it would still be easy to choose a case.

   B. *Are You Smarter Than a 5th Grader?* The questions on this show are usually pretty easy. Plus, they give you three safety nets and you can drop out whenever you want (not that you would).

   C. *Family Feud.* Coming up with answers on the spot would be a piece of cake for you. And you just know you'd rock the speed round at the end.

   D. *Million Dollar Password.* The whole game is a race against time. You have to give great clues or guess your partner's— all while listening to the clock tick away. Only people who are able to keep their cool do well on that show, and let's just say you'd leave with the grand prize.

3. **If you had to choose, you'd be**:

   A. a yoga instructor. Half your job is teaching people how to reeelaaax. And the clothes are pretty comfy too. You don't even have to wear shoes! Talk about stress free . . .

B. a midwife. True, there is a bit of tension involved (you are helping to bring a new baby into the world, after all!) but your focus on meditation and creating a soothing atmosphere for the mom-to-be makes this a fairly mellow job.

C. a fashion-magazine editor's assistant, like Anne Hathaway in *The Devil Wears Prada*. Some girls might shy away from a job that has you running around in heels all day and night, doing a million things at once, but it looks exciting to you! Besides, when you get to enjoy some downtime, you'll be doing it in Gucci and Jimmy Choos. Totally worth the stress!

D. an ER doctor. You don't get much more high-pressure than this job. You'd get no sleep, you'd be on call twenty-four seven, and you'd have only split seconds to make life-saving decisions. The upside? You'd save a lot of people.

4. **You have a big science project due at the end of the year. You:**

A. start months and months in advance. That way you can do a little bit every day and not get overwhelmed. Why procrastinate when you could be done by Thanksgiving and not have to worry about it after that?

B. get started at least a month or so before it's due. As long as you set up a careful schedule for yourself and stick to it, you should be done just in time without breaking a sweat.

C. procrastinate until a week before it's due. You work best under pressure—or so you tell yourself. By now most of the good ideas are taken and your parents have to help you scramble for supplies, but that's all part of the fun . . . not.

D. start working on it the day it's due and end up having to beg your teacher for more time. You'll lose a letter grade and will have to sweat bullets to get it in before you fail altogether, but that date just snuck up on you!

5. **You run into your crush unexpectedly at the mall, and he says hi. You:**

A. say something that sounds like "Uh . . . um . . . h-hi . . . urgh . . ." Unfortunately, your tongue always seems to tie itself into knots whenever you're around someone you like. Better just wave at him from far away next time.

B. say, "Hey," nervously, then run away like your sneakers are on fire. You're lucky you got out one word. Stay any longer and you risk serious humiliation.

C. say hi and ask him about the homework assignment from class. Maybe it's not the most stimulating conversation, but you're pretty comfortable talking about school, so it's a good way to stay calm in the face of unbelievable cuteness.

D. tell him a great joke you just heard and flirt away. Even though you weren't expecting to see him today, you immediately snap into your most practiced notice-me moves.

Give yourself 1 point for every time you answered **A**, 2 points for every **B**, 3 points for every **C**, and 4 points for every **D**.
   —If you scored between 5 and 12, turn to page 210.
   —If you scored between 13 and 20, turn to page 194.

chapter ELEVEN

Wow, Blair Waldorf has nothing on you! When it comes to getting what you want, you don't mind being downright ruthless. Or is that just what you think you have to do to win? Although you do tend to get your way in the short term, eventually your hard-core methods will backfire. Remember, what goes around comes around.

Before you can face going out on the set and dealing with Mona, you need to call your friends and see what's happening in the real world. You flip open your phone and hit the speed-dial key for Jessie. It barely rings once before she answers.

"Hey, supermodel! How's it going in the glamorous world of high fashion? Has *Access Hollywood* shown up to document your rise to stardom? Have they whisked you off to Paris yet?"

"No such luck," you say, glancing around the dim back room of the Photo Hut. "But wait till you see the gear they have me wearing. It's unreal."

"Oh, you're so lucky!" Jessie exclaims. "Bebe LaRue's clothes are fabtastic. I'm so jealous."

"Me too!" you hear Lena call just above the tinny sound of Elvis singing "All Shook Up" in the background.

"Hey, are you guys at Johnny Rockets?" It's the only place you know of in the mall that has those table juke-boxes filled entirely with songs from the fifties and sixties. "Now *I'm* jealous."

"Well, get used to it, Tyra. If you want to be a big-time model, that means no more greasy hamburgers and high-fat milk shakes. From now on, it's all about fruit, vegetables, whole grains, tofu—"

"Oh, I am *so* outta here," you interrupt. "I was with you right until the tofu. Blegh."

"Don't you dare move a muscle, young lady," Jessie says, doing her best impression of your mom. "I'm counting on you to make lots of friends there so you can eventually introduce me to that hot male model we saw in *Teen Vogue* last month."

You have to laugh. "You got it. Hey, did you hear about Lizette winning a ticket to the party?"

"Of course," Jessie replies. "Amy works faster than e-mail spam. I think she called everybody. But Lizette isn't the only one. When Lena and I were carrying Jimmy here, we ran into Charlie and he told us that—"

"Back up!" you interrupt again. "Jimmy's with you guys?"

"Oh. Did I forget to mention that?" Jessie says calmly. You're sure she's fully aware that she is torturing you.

"Yeah, it must've slipped your mind. Spill it, Jess!" you cry impatiently.

"It's not a big deal, really," Jessie starts, still talking too slowly for your taste. "After you took off, Lena and I ran to find a quiet place so we could call your mom. But Shakespeare here decides to update her blog while in motion and ends up in a head-on collision with Jimmy. Poor guy never saw it coming."

"Hey, you could have warned me!" Lena protests in the background.

Ignoring her, Jessie continues, "He was pretty woozy after she brutally crashed into him—"

"Do you have to say it like that? It was an accident! Sheesh . . ."

"Pipe down over there, Lena. I'm telling the story," Jessie says, clearly finding the whole scenario hilarious. "As I was saying, he was pretty woozy after . . . the accident." You picture Jessie putting air quotes around "accident." "So we did what any good EMTs would do and got him twenty CCs of chocolate milk, stat."

You can hear Jimmy and Lena chuckling in the background.

"It was touch and go there for a while, but I think he'll make it. Say hi, Jimmy," Jessie continues.

"Hi, Jimmy," he says. *Could this be any more perfect?* you think. Here you were, wondering what to do about Mona, and now your friends are hanging out with her date. It gives you a great idea.

"Wow," you say once Jessie is back on the line. "This is a really weird day. You'll never believe who's at the photo shoot with me."

Sensing juicy gossip, Jessie gets excited. "I'll be right back, guys," she announces to Jimmy and Lena, and you hear the background music slowly subside. She must have walked outside of the diner so she could hear you better. "Who? Who?" she asks.

"Mona. And unless I completely heard wrong, Janice is Mona's mom ... and Jimmy is her date to Shawna's party."

There is a moment of stunned silence before Jessie yelps, "What?"

"I know. Crazy, right? The Truth or Dare promise I made is so off." You silently thank God that you didn't get the chance to ask Jimmy out on a date earlier. He would have had to turn you down cold and the cringe factor of that moment would have been epic.

"Get out! That can't be true. Are you sure you got that right?"

"Definitely." You leave out the part about your eaves-dropping to get that info.

Jessie groans. "Aw, this bites. I'm sooo sorry. This is just like what happened on *Ugly Betty* that time—"

"Hey, Jess," you interrupt, "would you mind if we saved the *Ugly Betty* recap for later? I can't stay on the phone too long."

"Yeah. No problem. But are you sure you're okay?"

You think about it for a moment, surprised to find that you *are* okay. "I am," you assure Jessie. "I know I should be more miserable right now, but the truth is . . . I think I may have met someone else." An image of Bryan pops into your mind. Of course Jessie demands all the details, but before you have a chance to fill her in, you notice the time. If you want your plan to work, you've got to get moving . . . *now*.

"I'll tell you all about it later," you say in a rush. "Just take your time at Johnny Rockets. Have some fries on me."

"You'll get no argument here, Ms. Klum."

After you get off the phone, you innocently stroll out to where Mona is sitting on the set, impatiently tapping her foot.

"Hey, Mona," you say brightly, getting a snotty eye roll from her in return. Okay, guess this won't be as easy as you thought. You really, really hate this, but you're going to have to do the unspeakable: give Mona a compliment to get her talking.

"Your hair looks hot," you say, swallowing extra hard so you won't accidentally hurl. "How do you get it to look so shiny? It's like you should be in Pantene commercials."

Mona looks sideways at you, clearly a bit suspicious.

"Are you serious?"

"Yeah!" you assure her. You grab a chunk of your own hair. "I'm amazed they could do anything with mine. It usually feels like straw. Yours probably feels like silk. What's your secret?"

Mona sizes you up a final time and seems to decide that you're being for real. "For starters, I use leave-in conditioner and brush it through my hair for *at least* fifteen minutes," she confides.

It worked! You pegged her just right. A queen bee like Mona can't resist a fawning captive audience. Before long, she's telling you all kinds of stuff . . . like how she was in Babies "R" Us catalogs when she was one year old and has been working ever since, how girls at school are all just jealous of her, and how Jimmy, her escort to Shawna's party, is in the mall somewhere waiting for her as she speaks.

You see your opening and go for it.

"Yeah, my friends called me a minute ago and said they saw Jimmy at Johnny Rockets. But I didn't know you were taking him to the party. You guys will look so cute together!" It hurts to even say that, because of course you think *you* and Jimmy would have made a much cuter pair. But now that you've met Bryan, you aren't so sure how you feel about Jimmy. And right now you gotta do what you gotta do.

"I know," Mona says. God, she's conceited. "It just bites that I have to be here right now instead of with him, picking out our outfits. I mean, all this waiting around is what you make the newbies do, not professionals like me."

"You're so right," you say, egging her on. "In fact, why don't you head over to Johnny Rockets and surprise him? Steve told me the shoot was going to be delayed by at least twenty minutes, so you have plenty of time." Okay, that's a total lie, but you have your fingers crossed behind your back, so it doesn't count.

Mona looks a little hesitant. For all her bravado, she is obviously as scared of ticking off Janice as everyone else is. "Um . . . I don't know. . . ."

"Oh." You shrug. "I understand. You have to take orders just like the rest of us. My bad. I thought you were, like, the star of the show."

Mona's clear blue eyes take on the hard look that Janice has perfected. "Of *course* I'm the star of the show."

"If that's true," you answer, blinking innocently, "it's not like we can start the shoot without you anyway . . . right?"

Mona puffs out her chest and raises her chin. "That's right," she says, then stands up. "I'm going to find Jimmy. And if I decide to take longer than twenty minutes, the photographers will just have to hold their horses!"

You actually clap for her as she leaves, feeding her ego even more. You're not sure your friends would approve of what you just did, but in this case, you think the ends justify the means. Mona is gone and you don't have to deal with her constant snarky remarks. Plus, you might have a shot now at ruling this photo shoot. *Teen Vogue,* here you come!

A couple of minutes later, Janice emerges from the back room, announcing that it is time to get started. "Models, take your places!" she yells. You all file onto the set, which basically consists of some large white squares in front of a background that's all white except for some gold spray-painted leaves scattered around the floor. The main photographer comes out to arrange the models the way he wants them. The first set of pictures will be group shots, so there are lines of tape on the floor to indicate your marks — where you all need to stand to be in the frame. You are nervous, but excited, positive that with Mona out of the way, you'll totally steal the spotlight.

But just as you're thinking that, Janice scans the group and says, "Mona? Where's Mona?" Her eyes land on you. You could tell her the truth, but you start thinking about the mean things Mona does all the time. She always cuts in the lunch line. She's pulled the gum-on-your-seat move more than once. And she even made fun of Andy Grain's weight. She's a total nightmare. How she ended up hanging with sweet, quiet Jimmy, you have no idea, but you know for sure that he can do better. You could take the high road here, but instead you look right into Janice's eyes, shrug, and say, "Beats me." This could quite possibly be the most evil thing you've ever done, but come on. Mona deserves it . . . doesn't she?

Janice's face turns an angry shade of red, and her lips purse into a hard, tight line. Whoa, she seriously looks like she's about to flip her lid. "I need some air, Jean Paul," she tells the photographer. "Go ahead and get started."

She angrily stomps out into the hall, heading for the exit. The photographer looks a little unsure at first, but then he starts snapping away. Unfortunately, everyone seems on edge after Janice's stormy exit. "I said elongate your neck!" Jean Paul keeps telling the model next to you, a really cute guy named Elliott, who you recognize from a couple of magazines. "And you—you're stepping out of frame." None of you seem to be doing that well.

And by the time Janice comes back in, having calmed down a little, Mona is standing in the doorway. Not good. Not good at all. What is she doing back so soon? She takes one look at the set and realizes that the shoot has started without her. She glances your way for just a second, but you know you're in for it. It's pretty obvious you lied to her.

"Thanks for gracing us with your presence," Janice says to Mona sarcastically. Jean Paul quits clicking immediately.

Mona looks at the floor, clenching her fists as if she's barely able to contain her anger. "Chill, Mom. I just had to run to get some water. It won't happen again."

"Make sure it doesn't," Janice snaps. "Or else this will be your last job with Bebe LaRue. Now get on set!"

"Okay, okay," Mona says, holding up her hands. She steps onto the white set, shoving in between you and Elliott. For a moment you think maybe she isn't even mad at you. After all, she could have ratted you out to Janice just now, but she didn't.

But then she leans over and whispers in your ear, "You'll pay for that." And when she pulls away, she is shooting you some serious death glares.

Before you know it, the shoot is back on, and Mona is more determined than ever to box you out of it. And this time, you're not entirely sure that you don't deserve it.

Frame after frame, Mona's hands end up in front of your face, or she steps on your foot, causing you to bend over in pain just before the photo snaps. And the whole time, she keeps stepping just a little to the left, slowly but surely pushing you to the other side of the tape so that you're not in the shot at all. The worst part is Jean Paul doesn't even seem to notice!

So much for your big career in modeling. And from the look on Janice's face, you can tell you can kiss those Graphic Art Museum wrap-party passes good-bye too. You won't give Mona the satisfaction of seeing you cry, but you have to admit you've been outplayed. The icing on the cake is that you have to face your friends as anything but America's Next Top Model. Great.

Hate to say this, but ruthlessness is not a good look for you. Your desire to teach Mona a lesson is understandable, but all you managed to do was start a war. And Mona has been playing the ruthless game way longer than you have. So now you've blown your big modeling break and let yourself down in a major way. Hopefully things are going better for Jessie and Lena. But if they are, can you put aside your own frustration at how your day turned out and be happy for your friends? Take the quiz and see.

QUIZ TIME!

Circle your answers and tally up the points at the end.

1. **Your friend comes to school with yet another brand-new Coach bag. You:**

    A. feel extremely annoyed. You don't have even one Coach bag, let alone a dozen. It feels like she's just rubbing it in your face.

    B. are kind of jealous. Your friend always has the nicest things, while you are still rocking your older sister's hand-me-downs. You're glad for your friend but are upset that it never seems to be your turn.

    C. feel a little embarrassed that you don't have bags as nice as hers. But it's always good to see her happy.

D. are in awe of your friend's hot sense of style. You're thrilled she got another bag! Just being seen with someone who owns one of those makes you feel glamorous. And if you're lucky, maybe she'll lend it to you!

2. **You've always been the youngest in the family, but your mom just had a baby. You:**

   A. hate it. Say good-bye to all the special attention you used to get. Now it's baby, baby, baby every single day. The only time anyone seems to remember your name anymore is when your folks want you to change some poopy diapers.

   B. could do without it. Nothing against babies or anything, but this business about skipping family game night just so you can take yet another home video of the baby? Lame.

   C. feel like it's growing on you. You're not quite sure yet if you're going to like sharing the spotlight, but how could you help loving that tiny little face? Clearly the baby's an evil genius.

   D. love it. You even offer to give up your own room so the baby can have more space. And you're always the first one to volunteer to change the dirty diapers. All a part of being a big sis.

3. **You try out for a plum spot on the soccer team, but another girl is given the star forward spot you wanted, while you're stuck warming the bench. You:**

   A. quit the team. What's the point of being here if you're going to spend all your time sitting on the sidelines? And

146

who wants to play for a coach who can't recognize talent when he sees it?

B. grumble on the bench to anyone who will listen. Somebody has to hear about what an injustice was done on the field. And you're sure they'll all agree with you.

C. mope about it in silence. You don't agree with what the coach did, but what he says goes, so there's nothing you can do about it anyway. Might as well just try your best to put your feelings aside and support the team.

D. become the loudest bench-warming cheerleader there is. You even offer to wear a goofy mascot costume. If you can't help your teammates by being on the field, you can at least boost their spirits like crazy!

4. **A boy you've been dating, Jake, has a friend who is going through a rough time at home, and she has started calling him to talk about it. You:**

A. forbid him to talk to her anymore and start monitoring his phone calls just in case. You know that his friend is dealing with something, but you don't want her spending too much time with Jake. You seriously doubt she just wants to be his friend.

B. feel bad for her, but don't exactly trust her motives, and you tell Jake so. Maybe you're putting him in an awkward position, but that's just how you feel.

C. are a little uneasy about it, but you don't want Jake to think you don't trust him. You keep your reservations to yourself but keep an eye on his friend all the same.

D. feel so sorry for her that you encourage Jake to spend more time with her. They're friends, after all. If you were in her position, you would hope that Jake would be there for you.

5. **You're a big pop star and are up for a Grammy this year. But the award goes to a newcomer who is being called the next big thing. You:**

A. are furious! How could she have won over you? Are those judges deaf? You storm out and vow to boycott all future awards shows.

B. clap and smile but are secretly fuming inside. You know for a fact that your album was way better than hers, but there's no accounting for taste.

C. are a little disappointed, but you've heard her album and it isn't half bad. There's always next year.

D. are happy just to have been nominated. You tell the reporters she deserved it. She obviously worked hard and is super-talented.

Give yourself 1 point for every time you answered **A**, 2 points for every **B**, 3 points for every **C**, and 4 points for every **D**.

—If you scored between 5 and 12, go to page 234.

—If you scored between 13 and 20, go to page 224.

chapter TWELVE

Brava! You're nobody's doormat. When someone tries to take advantage of you, you don't stand for it. In fact, you make your voice heard loud and clear. You'd make a great lawyer or political activist. But choose your battles wisely. Not every situation calls for you to jump down someone's throat.

After Steve heads up to the front to talk to the head photographer, Jean Paul, you pull the curtain back and check out the set. It is all white with a few large white cubes in the center. The only spots of color are the spray-painted gold leaves scattered across the floor. Against that background, the glammed-up models, all dressed in shades of blue, brown, and other earth tones, really stand out—especially the very pouty Mona, who, despite being such a nightmare, looks great. Her jet-black hair, falling on the sides of her face in gentle waves, and her alabaster skin and soft pink lips make her look like a doll or an angel. If you didn't know her, and if Bryan hadn't just given you an earful about her, you might think Mona was sweet. Too bad she's such an obnoxious diva.

Then again, you do feel kind of sorry for her. After all, it couldn't have been easy growing up with Janice as her mom. Janice doesn't exactly seem like the nurturing type. And you guess that if you had been doing the modeling thing for a while, like Mona, it would be pretty easy to get caught up in the lifestyle and start believing that you're more fabulous than everyone else. Admit it: You've been a model for only about two hours, and already you're this close to demanding a bowl of red-only M&M'S, and you have a hankering for fancy French coffee—and you don't even drink coffee! You could easily turn into Kimora Lee Simmons—the epitome of a demanding woman living the fab life—if you didn't have friends like Lena and Jessie, who will let you know in a heartbeat when you're River-dancing on their last nerve, and then make you laugh about it. Does Mona have anybody like that in her life? You doubt it. Maybe she just needs some more down-to-earth friends.

Still, that's no excuse for her being a total jerk, and maybe the other suck-ups in her posse don't care how she acts, but you're not going to let her treat you however she wants. Time for some tough love.

You straighten your back and head over to the edge of the stage, where Mona is sitting. "Hey," you say to her. "How's it going?"

Mona looks up at you and rolls her eyes, "It would be going better if *you* weren't here."

"Oh well. Sucks to be you, then, 'cause I'm not going anywhere." You smile. "It just looked like maybe you needed some company."

"Ha!" Mona says, smirking at you. "Like I don't know why you're trying to be all buddy-buddy with me."

"Because I'm a glutton for punishment?" you offer. At the moment, that sounds like the only reasonable explanation.

"Noooo . . . ," Mona says like she's talking to a kindergartner. "You think if you can become my best friend, then I'll help you get signed with an agency or something and you can be just like me. What a user. So typical!"

"Whoa, whoa, whoaaa," you interrupt. "First of all, I already have a best friend. Two of 'em, actually. And secondly, I'm not the one who asked to be here. Your mom came and got me, remember? I'm not exactly stalking you. So you can just go ahead and get over yourself right now. And by the way, I'm pumped about getting to be a model today, but between you and me"—you lean in and whisper in Mona's ear—"I was just kind of hoping they'd let me keep the clothes."

When you pull away, you see that her face has softened up just a touch. "Soo . . . you really don't want anything from me?"

"Well, I could use a piece of gum if you have one, but other than that, no."

"Oh," she says, looking a bit uncomfortable. "Well, I don't chew gum. It makes you look like a cow."

"Right." You should have seen that one coming. She only uses gum as a weapon. "So . . . your friends must be psyched about knowing a model, huh?"

"Pfff," Mona grunts. "I don't have any friends around here."

You're not sure you believe her. You may have thought she was too toxic to hang with, but at school Mona always rolls with an entourage. "What about all the people I see you with at school?"

"Leeches," Mona answers quickly. "You know Lisa Topple?" You nod. "Well, the first time I invited her over to my house, I told her to bring movies or something. Instead, she brought a packet of headshots and spent the whole time talking to my mom."

"Ouch."

"Exactly. And that wasn't the first time that's happened. But whatever. I'm used to it now. It doesn't bother me."

"Riiight," you say slowly. "That's why you bit my head off before—because you're so cool with people entering your territory."

Mona folds her arms haughtily and fixes her big blue

eyes on you. "Look, you don't see me coming down to the soccer field trying to take over your little . . . playtime or whatever, do you? You have that turf. This one is mine."

"You know," you say, taking a seat next to her, "with aggression like that, you *should* be on the soccer team with me. Why don't you try out? Or at least hang out with us after the games?"

She looks at you and smirks again. "Yeah, right. As if I have time for after-school activities! While you guys are out playing in the dirt"—she wrinkles her nose—"I'm usually off posing for a catalog or getting new headshots or going to fabulous industry parties." She counts each item off on a finger while she looks up at the ceiling. "So I really don't have time to 'hang out,' but I don't expect you to understand." She pats your back condescendingly. Her face has *You're lucky I'm even talking to you* written all over it.

Yep, she's still a brat. But at least you kind of get her now. Her mom's a beast, she doesn't have any real friends, and she's always working. (Hmmm . . . if that's the modeling life, maybe it isn't for you after all.) She may act as if she's above all that "kid stuff" like having fun and hanging out with friends, but she's not fooling you for a second. You've never met somebody more in need of an emergency Johnny Rockets milk shake and maybe one of Jessie's famous sleepovers.

"Models!" you hear Janice call. "Everyone take your places on the set . . . *now!*"

Mona huffs and stands up. "Duty calls."

"Hey, look," you say as you stand up next to her. "I know you must have some *fab*ulous party to go to next Saturday or you're meeting with Benny Ninja to work on your posing or something, but if you can get out of it, it would be really cool if you would come over to Jessie's house with Lena and me for a sleepover. We'll just be giving each other facials, watching scary movies, pigging out on pizza . . . you know, the usual. But maybe you could come anyway and teach us how you do that French twist thing with your hair. We're hopeless when it comes to hairstyling."

Mona looks genuinely shocked. Her eyes are so wide that her fake lashes are batting against her perfectly trimmed brows. And you could be imagining this, but she seems to be tearing up a little. For a second there, it looks like she is going to give a very touching speech about how she's longed for real friends and can't wait to come over and braid your hair. But in a flash, she regains her composure and clears her throat. "Puh-leeease. I get my facials done at a spa, I hate scary movies, and I don't eat pizza."

Ah yes, there's the Mona you know and loathe. Still, you must have earned some kind of begrudging respect, because at least she stops looking at you like you're a dog turd.

"Look," she says, putting her hands on her waist. "We have to work together, so we might as well just get it over with. You're . . . kind of pretty, I guess, but you don't know anything about modeling. So just follow my lead so you don't make us all look bad. Agreed?"

154

That's as good an offer as you're going to get from Mona, so you take it. "Agreed."

You smile, secretly suspecting that there is a human in there after all. Way, way in there.

By the time the two of you take your places among all the other models, you wouldn't say you were friends. But you at least understand each other. You get that Mona isn't going to change anytime soon, and she gets that you aren't going to be run out of there like a dog with its tail between its legs. So when Jean Paul starts clicking away, the two of you feed off each other's vibes. Mona even gives you a few tips between shots to help you stand out more. At the end you even do one pose with the two of you standing back to back with your arms crossed and your faces aimed defiantly toward the light. It's fierce, if you do say so yourself. Everyone agrees that for a first-timer, you killed it in all the photos. Even Janice is impressed. Not that she says that, of course.

"Good," Janice snaps. "That was not a total disaster."

You can tell that Janice isn't used to complimenting people, so you'll take what you can get. But after how great you and her daughter just did, you think maybe you'll get a warmer reception from Mona.

"Mona, that was awesome! We totally rocked that shoot!" You reach up for a high five.

But Mona just stares at your hand as if she thinks you have a horrible disease called dorkitis and it's contagious. "Uh . . . I think you mean *I* rocked that shoot. You were just along for the ride. Now, if you'll get out of my way, I need to go find Jimmy." Without another word, she struts past you, flipping her hair in your face as she goes. Oh well. Same old Mona. But even her attitude-with-a-capital-*A* can't ruin your buzz. Right now you feel like a real-life supermodel. Move over, Tyra. Here comes the next big thing!

Later, after you pick up the passes to the wrap party from Steve (score!), change back into your old clothes, and hang up the designer duds in the wardrobe case (no, they're not letting you keep them), you hear a familiar voice say, "Not bad, new girl."

You turn to see Bryan standing just outside the changing room, leaning on his skateboard as if it's a really cool cane.

"What? You were watching the shoot?"

"Oh, the modeling stuff? Yeah, I saw some of that. But I was talking about the way you handled Mona. I heard what you said to her. That was"—he shrugs—"kind of cool. I wish Alexa had stood up to her like that."

You give him a half smile. "Yeah?"

"Yeah," he answers, looking down at his board. "Hey, let me see your phone for a second."

"O-kaaay," you say, not sure why he would want to see your Sidekick. He flips it open and quickly dials some numbers into it.

"There, now you know where to find me if you and your friends ever want to hang," he says, blowing his hair out of his face.

You smile happily as you take back your phone. You can't be sure, but you think your actions today just earned you Bryan's official seal of approval. Nice.

That was very impressive, missy! You handled Mona in a way that was both tough and kind, and as a result you had a killer photo shoot. Not to mention you now have in your possession tickets to the all-important Bebe LaRue wrap party at the museum. As if that weren't enough, Mona said you were pretty (even if it killed her to admit it), and Bryan seems to have dubbed you cool enough to hang out with. You are definitely riding the high right now. But are you the type to let your good fortune go to your head? Don't be so quick to answer! Only the quiz knows for sure. . . .

QUIZ TIME!

Circle your answers and tally up the points at the end.

1. **In group pictures, you tend to stand:**
   A. front and center. The most beautiful thing in a photo should always be in the middle so that your eye goes right to it. Cheese!
   B. a little off to the side. You don't want to hog the spotlight. But you do make it a point to wear a bit of red so you're sure to be noticed.
   C. in the back, off to the side. Preferably behind someone

else. Is it really necessary to have photographic evidence that you have a terrible haircut?

D. out of the frame. You try to avoid being in pictures whenever possible. The fewer eyes on you, the better.

2. **When you're on the phone with friends, you spend most of your time talking about:**

A. yourself. Your life is always so fascinating and you know that your friends like to live vicariously through you. True, you're usually the one calling them, but that's probably just because they assume you're out doing something fabulous and aren't home.

B. mostly yourself, but you usually remember to ask them how they're doing right before you hang up. They don't have as much going on as you, but you don't want them to feel left out.

C. mostly them. You give them a quick update, but you already know what's going on with you, so where's the fun in rehashing it for an hour? You'd rather hear what you missed.

D. them. Whatever's going on with them is usually way more interesting than your ho-hum life. How often can you tell your friends the same ol' stories? You'd rather be the fascinated audience.

3. **A boy in your algebra class is staring at you. It probably means:**

A. he's in love with you. Duh. And can you blame him? You're sure he's never seen a girl quite as special as you are.

B. he likes you. You've caught him checking you out before, but he's probably too shy to say anything.

C. he wants to ask you what you got for number three. He knows algebra is your best subject, so he probably wants to make sure he got the right answer.

D. you have something in your teeth. You're positive that's it and he's about to laugh and tell all his friends that you must have had spinach for lunch. Great.

4. **A girl in your dance class doesn't seem to like you that much. It's probably because:**

A. she's jealous. You have the best dance skills in the class and she knows it. You can't help it if you're a better dancer than she is. Sheesh!

B. she doesn't know you very well. If she did, she'd know that you are definitely a friend worth having.

C. you haven't gone out of your way to talk to her. But that's only because you're kind of shy, which people sometimes mistake as being rude.

D. you probably stepped on her foot by accident during rehearsal. You do sometimes have two left feet.

5. **If you were on a reality show like *The City*, you'd expect to be:**

A. the star of the show. The camera loves you, and your friends' lives usually revolve around you anyway. And you have the perfect voice to be the narrator.

B. one of the major players. But being the star would take up too much of your time. You'd rather just show up for all the party scenes.

C. a guest star. It would be fun to be on the show once in a while, but it would be a lot of pressure to make your life seem exciting all the time. Cameos are definitely the way to go. That way no one gets sick of seeing you.

D. in a few quick scenes, but that's about it. Why would people want to watch your life? Zzzzzz . . .

Give yourself 1 point for every time you answered *A*, 2 points for every *B*, 3 points for every *C*, and 4 points for every *D*.
   —If you scored between 5 and 12, go to page 256.
   —If you scored between 13 and 20, go to page 261.

chapter THIRTEEN

From Chapter Six: You know only too well that what you put out into the universe tends to come back to you, so you try extra hard not to rock your karmic boat. When given the choice, you tend to do the right thing.

From Chapter Seven: Being around you is pretty relaxing, because you don't like to make waves. Unfortunately, you let people get away with murder because of that. You haven't quite yet realized that being a good person doesn't mean letting others walk all over you. You deserve as much respect as you give everyone else. But if you don't believe that, no one else will either.

After you hang up with Amy, you pull back the curtain a little and peek out at the set. It looks beautiful—just a plain white backdrop with a few giant white cubes in the middle and some gold spray-painted leaves scattered across the floor. Against that background, the models, all dressed in different shades of fall colors and earth tones, really pop. And since most of them are blond, Mona—with her jet-black hair and shimmery pink lipstick—really stands out. Well, it's either her hair or the fact that she's pacing back and forth with her arms crossed and steam coming out of her ears. She reminds you of a bull in a rodeo right after it sees the color red.

You know you should probably go out there and talk to her, but you can think of a million things you'd rather do.

Things You'd Rather Do
Than Confront Mona

- Go to school wearing My Little Pony pajamas.
- Scrub all the toilets in the mall . . . with your toothbrush.
- Have someone read your diary over the PA system.
- Drink a whole carton of spoiled milk.

It's safe to say confrontation is not your thing. You just want to model and have a good time. But why did she have to be here? You sigh and try to shake it off. Bottom line, Mona isn't going anywhere and neither are you, so you might as well just try to get through it.

After taking a few deep breaths, you walk out onto the set, where the photographer, Jean Paul, is arranging all the models. He puts you on the left-hand side and adjusts one of the large umbrellas until the light is hitting you just so.

"Remember," he warns you with a faint French accent, "you need to stay within the frame."

You hate to sound stupid, but you have no idea what he means. "Um, the frame?" you ask.

Jean Paul sighs and shakes his head. "Yes, the frame." He holds up his hands in front of him, making Ls with his index fingers and thumbs. "This is what I see in my camera. If you are standing outside of it, you will not be in the picture. Look down."

You do as you're told and see that there are lines of tape on the floor, forming three sides of a rectangle.

"Those are your marks. Step outside of those and you don't exist. Got it?"

"Got it . . . I think." Okay, you're a smart girl and normally you wouldn't need this explained to you as if you were five. But right now you are shaking in your three-hundred-dollar flats and can hardly think straight. The truth is you're on the verge of a major freak-out.

"Don't worry," a syrupy voice says beside you. Mona has stopped her angry pacing and is standing next to you now.

She throws one arm around your shoulders. "I'll show her the ropes, Jean Paul."

"Excellent," he says, obviously relieved.

As he goes about positioning the tripod and testing the lights, you whisper to Mona, "Thanks for the save. Very cool of you. I guess I'm just a little nervous. Any advice for me?"

Mona leans in close to your ear and whispers, "Yeah. Stay out of my way."

You pull back and stare at her sneering face. Ah, now *there's* the Mona you're used to. "What?"

"You heard me. It's bad enough I had to waste so much time here this morning, waiting for you. But if you think I'm going to let an *amateur* from the *mall* take over my shoot, you're dumber than you look."

Your mouth just hangs open in what Jessie would call fly-catching position. Did she really just say that? To you? Now you're fuming. If this is what Alexa had to put up with all that time, you can understand why she bailed. There are a million ways you could react—half of which would probably land you in jail. But you're really too shocked to do much of anything.

Suddenly you hear Jean Paul snapping away. The other models are making small adjustments—shifting a leg here, moving an arm up there—and you're doing your best to follow their lead. But Mona takes the cake. True to her word, she lets you know this really is *her* shoot. Just before one shot, she tosses her long black hair to the left, right into your face. In another she takes what looks like a superhero stance, hands on her hips and her legs spread in a wide V, forcing you to move off to the side. Five more shots go by before you look down and realize that you're standing outside the taped line. Great. You'll be lucky if your elbow shows up in any of those frames, let alone your face. You picture your whole life as a model—the great clothes, the famous friends, fashion week at Bryant Park—swirling down a giant drain.

Before you know it, the shoot is over and Jean Paul is thanking everyone for their time. Mona flounces away with one last smirk in your direction. Unreal! She already stole your dream of showing up at Shawna's place with Jimmy, and now she's ruined your one chance at being a model. And she isn't the least bit sorry!

You stand there in a state of total disbelief for the longest time.

Finally Steve comes up to you, clipboard in hand. He kind of winces and says, "Yeah, that didn't go too well for you, honey."

"Thank you, Captain Obvious," you snap. Nothing better than getting humiliated and then having someone point it out. Still, Steve has been nothing but nice to you. He didn't deserve that. "Sorry," you mumble. "It's just . . ."

"I know, I know," he says, patting your arm. "That's all right. But there are two more things I need to tell you."

You look up at him, thinking he's going to request a hug to make you feel better and tell you how beautiful you are. Aw, he's sweet.

"Well, Janice should really be telling you this, but she watched the shoot and . . . well, she's decided to auction off the passes to the wrap party."

Ouch. You forgot all about the wrap party for a second. But now that Steve has reminded you, all you can think about is how badly you wanted those passes . . . and why. "Fine," you say grouchily. "What's the other thing?"

"Okay, I really hate to mention it, but . . . those clothes you're wearing aren't part of the deal. The garment bag is in the changing room." Then he does give you a quick hug. "Better luck next time, sweetheart."

Oh. You can almost hear Lena quoting Shakespeare at you right now. *This was the most unkindest cut of all . . ."* You head back to the small changing room and carefully hang your Bebe LaRue wardrobe back in the garment bag. You slide on your jeans and T-shirt and beat-up Nikes, and the transformation back into your old self is complete. Could this day have gone any worse?

Almost as if the universe is answering your question, your phone rings. When you flip it open, you hear a crowd of people cheering and clapping. The noise is so loud that you have to hold the phone away from your ear.

"I woooooon!" someone screams.

"Lena? Is that you?"

"Yes! Can you believe it? I won!"

"That's awesome!" you say, trying your best to muster up some enthusiasm. "What did you have to do?"

"Well, I found Shawna at the movie theater. She was behind the counter, scooping out popcorn. So I had to answer a bunch of trivia questions about Reese Witherspoon movies and then I had to eat a small bucket of popcorn in one minute flat. And I did it!"

The crowd behind her cheers again. Hey, actually, this *is* awesome. You may have blown your chance to be a big-time model, but at least you still have Shawna's birthday to look forward to.

"Sweet!" you shout to Lena, now genuinely excited. "We get to go to the party together! This is so what I needed right now. You won't even believe what happened at the Photo Hut. . . ." You stop rambling when you realize that Lena is being especially quiet. "Lena, you still there?"

"Huh? Oh y-yeah . . . ," she stammers. "About that. Um. I kind of decided to take Jessie, since she's the one who practically forced me to watch *Legally Blonde*. If it weren't for her, I would have spent the summer watching *Masterpiece Theatre*. And she's the one who made us come here today in the first place. You understand, right?"

Sure, you understand. . . . You understand that you need new best friends! How could they do this to you after the kind of day you've had?

"Yeah, of course. No problem."

"Great," Lena says, breathing a sigh of relief. But then she kind of gurgles. "Uh-oh."

"What's wrong?" you ask.

"Oof . . . I think all that popcorn kind of made me sick. Ohh, in fact, I think I'm gonna be sick right now. . . . Gotta go!" The last thing you hear is Lena hurling into a trash can.

Which is actually kind of perfect, since that's what you feel like doing right about now. Instead, you gather up your stuff and start to make your way toward the exit when you find a tall object standing in your way. Bryan.

He has his arms folded and is shaking his head. "Why didn't you stand up to her?" he asks. "You just let her take over, as usual. That sucked."

You would defend yourself, tell him all about how hard it is to navigate the waters of preteen-girl drama, but you don't think he'd understand. And you're pretty sure you're about to cry, so you brush past him and get the heck out of there. Bad enough you let yourself down by not standing up to Mona. You don't really relish the thought of skater boy witnessing your meltdown.

Anybody who tells you that your modeling debut went well is a big fat liar. Not to be brutal, but that chapter bit big-time. Because you didn't stand up for yourself, Mona dominated what should have been your big break, and it cost you the passes to the wrap party. Not that it matters, since you haven't even seen Jimmy—who is inexplicably tight with

Mona—and any hope you had of getting to know Bryan better just went up in smoke. Need we even mention that Lena won tickets to Shawna's party and is taking Jessie instead of you? Yeah, you've had better moments. But what matters now is how you choose to cope. You have a lot of options, some better than others. Ask yourself honestly what you would do next. Better yet, let the quiz answer for you.

QUIZ TIME!

Circle your answers and tally up the points at the end.

1. **Your friend comes to school with yet another brand-new Coach bag. You:**
   - *A.* feel extremely annoyed. You don't have even one Coach bag, let alone a dozen. It feels like she's just rubbing it in your face.
   - *B.* are kind of jealous. Your friend always has the nicest things, while you are still rocking your older sister's hand-me-downs. You're glad for your friend but are upset that it never seems to be your turn.
   - *C.* feel a little embarrassed that you don't have bags as nice as hers. But it's always good to see her happy.
   - *D.* are in awe of your friend's hot sense of style. You're thrilled she got another bag! Just being seen with someone who owns one of those makes you feel glamorous. And if you're lucky, maybe she'll lend it to you!

2. **You've always been the youngest in the family, but your mom just had a baby. You:**

A. hate it. Say good-bye to all the special attention you used to get. Now it's baby, baby, baby every single day. The only time anyone seems to remember your name anymore is when your folks want you to change some poopy diapers.

B. could do without it. Nothing against babies or anything, but this business about skipping family game night just so you can take yet another home video of the baby? Lame.

C. feel like it's growing on you. You're not quite sure yet if you're going to like sharing the spotlight, but how could you help loving that tiny little face? Clearly the baby's an evil genius.

D. love it. You even offer to give up your own room so the baby can have more space. And you're always the first one to volunteer to change the dirty diapers. All a part of being a big sis.

3. **You try out for a plum spot on the soccer team, but another girl is given the star forward spot you wanted, while you're stuck warming the bench. You:**

A. quit the team. What's the point of being here if you're going to spend all your time sitting on the sidelines? And who wants to play for a coach who can't recognize talent when he sees it?

B. grumble on the bench to anyone who will listen. Somebody has to hear about what an injustice was done on the field. And you're sure they'll all agree with you.

C. mope about it in silence. You don't agree with what the coach did, but what he says goes, so there's nothing you can do about it anyway. Might as well just try your best to put your feelings aside and support the team.

D. become the loudest bench-warming cheerleader there is. You even offer to wear a goofy mascot costume. If you can't help your teammates by being on the field, you can at least boost their spirits like crazy!

4. **A boy you've been dating, Jake, has a friend who is going through a rough time at home, and she has started calling him to talk about it. You:**

A. forbid him to talk to her anymore and start monitoring his phone calls just in case. You know that his friend is dealing with something, but you don't want her spending too much time with Jake. You seriously doubt she just wants to be his friend.

B. feel bad for her, but don't exactly trust her motives, and you tell Jake so. Maybe you're putting him in an awkward position, but that's just how you feel.

C. are a little uneasy about it, but you don't want Jake to think you don't trust him. You keep your reservations to yourself but keep an eye on his friend all the same.

D. feel so sorry for her that you encourage Jake to spend more time with her. They're friends, after all. If you were in her position, you would hope that Jake would be there for you.

5. **You're a big pop star and are up for a Grammy this year. But the award goes to a newcomer who is being called the next big thing. You:**

   A. are furious! How could she have won over you? Are those judges deaf? You storm out and vow to boycott all future awards shows.

   B. clap and smile but are secretly fuming inside. You know for a fact that your album was way better than hers, but there's no accounting for taste.

   C. are a little disappointed, but you've heard her album and it isn't half bad. There's always next year.

   D. are happy just to have been nominated. You tell the reporters she deserved it. She obviously worked hard and is super-talented.

Give yourself 1 point for every time you answered *A*, 2 points for every *B*, 3 points for every *C*, and 4 points for every *D*.

—If you scored between 5 and 12, go to page 234.

—If you scored between 13 and 20, go to page 224.

chapter
FOURTEEN

Picasso, Shakespeare, Donna Karan . . . You might as well go ahead and add your name to this list, because you are creative and artistic, just like them. None of your friends would be at all surprised if you grew up to be a fashion designer, actress, playwright, sculptor, or dancer. All it takes is drive and imagination. Good thing you've got plenty of both.

The henna tattoo shop is one of your favorite places in the mall. It's the least lame, anyway. Aromatherapy candles light up the room instead of harsh fluorescent lights, there's always cool world music playing that you've never heard before, and there are henna patterns lining the walls. This place is so soothing (hopefully soothing enough to help you forget about Jimmy for a while). You remember from Shawna's Facebook page that she's a fan of henna tattoos. So you figure you might as well check here first.

Unfortunately, everyone *except* Shawna seems to be there.

"Lizette is taking *me*!" Delia screams in her high-pitched voice, wrecking the Zen vibe of the place.

"In your dreams," Celia yells back. "She's taking *me*."

"Me!"

"*Me!*"

"Would you guys shut up already?" Lizette breaks in. Her left leg is propped up on a red plastic chair, and the bored-looking woman sitting across from her is painting a henna design all around Lizette's ankle. "You're embarrassing me! Keep it up and I won't take either one of you!" She rolls her brown eyes at them before she notices you standing there. "Hey. Care to buy a twin? They're on sale today—two for the price of one. Going once, going twice . . ."

"Pass," you say. "I've had my eye on this set of newborn triplets that poop around the clock. You understand."

"Yeah," Lizette says, moaning a little. "I'd probably take some poopy triplets over these two knuckleheads right about now too. Here I thought winning a ticket to Shawna's party would be so cool, but they've been fighting over who gets to go with me ever since. *Ay, Dios mio,* it's driving me up the freakin' wall!"

You glance over at the dueling twins, who now have a small crowd of kids from school surrounding them and giggling. It is kind of funny, because the twins have exactly the same mannerisms and the same hairstyle, so it seems like Delia is looking into a mirror and yelling at herself.

"She should take me. I'm older than you!"

"Only by two minutes!"

You look back at Lizette with fresh sympathy. "Yeah, that's getting ugly," you tell her. "But at least your ankle is ready to party."

Lizette looks down at the finished henna design, with its swirling black lines crisscrossing her ankle. "Wow. Love it!" she says to the woman. "Would you accept one of the twins as payment? They do dishes. . . ."

"Cash only, please," the woman says, tapping the small sign next to her and totally missing the joke. "Next!"

Lizette pays the woman and stands up, careful not to smudge the new design on the edge of the chair. "You should get one. If you get to go to the party, it'll be the perfect accessory."

"Fat chance of that happening," you answer. "I feel like I've been wandering around this mall all day, and I haven't spotted Shawna once. What's a girl gotta do to get a golden ticket around here?" You picture Veruca Salt having her father's whole factory look through a sea of chocolate bars to find her one. Yeah, you'll have to call that Plan B.

Lizette gently pushes you down into the seat across from the humorless tattoo woman. "Don't worry about it for now. Shawna's around here somewhere and you're bound to run into her." She hands you a book full of henna designs. "Might as well go for a few extra cool points in the meantime. And these tattoos are so fly."

The girl makes good sense. You flip through the book quickly and decide on what looks like a butterfly pattern to go around your wrist when Gwen Stefani starts singing at your hip. It's your Sidekick, and that's your ringtone for Lena. Maybe she'll have some good news for you.

"Hey, Lena," you greet her. "What's shakin'?"

"Me!" she shouts back at you. *"I won!"* She is screaming so loudly you have to hold the phone away from you to protect your eardrum. Even at arm's length, you can hear a crowd of people cheering behind her. She goes on excitedly, "You know how I went to the movie theater, right? Well, it turns out she *was* at the movie theater! She was behind the concession stand, scooping popcorn. Mark tried to claim that he saw her first, but nobody was buying that. So Shawna told me I had to answer a bunch of questions about Reese Witherspoon movies and then eat a small bucket of popcorn in one minute flat. It wasn't the most dignified thing I've ever done. But I did it. I did it! Shawna took off right after, but now I've got a ticket! *Woohooo!"*

You jerk out of your chair, wrecking the design that was being carefully painted on your wrist—and really annoying the woman. But what do you care? One of your best friends just won a ticket! "That's awesome!" you cry. "That means we can go to the party! That's great, because I'm getting a henna tattoo right now that is going to look so good with this dress I bought last week. And after that whole Jimmy fiasco, the party will be the perfect pick-me-up and . . ."

You trail off when you realize that Lena is unusually quiet now.

"Uh . . . Lena? You still there?"

"Yeah, I'm here," she says hesitantly. "But, um . . . well, sorry I didn't mention this sooner, but I kind of decided to take Jessie. I mean, she is the one who practically tied me to a chair and forced me to watch *Legally Blonde*. Plus, she is the one who begged us to come to the mall. You're not mad at me, are you?"

You think about that for a moment and decide no. Lena is right. If not for Jessie, none of you would be at the mall today in the first place. She deserves to go to the party. Still, this means the odds of your winning a ticket just got even worse. But for her sake, you shove your disappointment away and do your best to sound cheerful.

"No, I'm not mad. In fact, I'll come meet up with you guys now and we can celebrate."

Lena lets out a relieved sigh. "Great! That would be so . . . oh, urgh . . ."

"Hey, what's wrong?" you ask.

"You know all that popcorn I ate? *Argh* . . . I think I'm gonna be sick. I think —"

And the last sound you hear before Lena hangs up is her hurling into the nearest trash can.

Next to you Lizette starts laughing. "Wow! Amy works fast!" She holds out her phone to show you a video message she just received of Lena bent over a trash can, puking her guts out.

"Sheesh," you say. "Poor Lena! Well, at least you can't see her face." Although you think that won't be much of a consolation to Lena. She's going to need something special to distract her when she realizes she was taped tossing her cookies. "Hey, Lizette, wanna ditch your cousins and come with me to buy Lena something to celebrate her big win?"

She sneaks a peek back at Celia and Delia, who are still bickering, although the crowd has long since gotten bored of the show and moved on. Without skipping a beat, she says, "Let's go."

As you head toward the movie theater, you see lots of kids from school, some proudly waving their golden tickets around, some shaking their heads. You hear Jasmine say to Charlie as they pass you by, "I can't believe I missed that one. The Aleutian Islands are in Alaska, not Antarctica. Stupid, stupid, stupid! Well, anyway, how are my teeth?"

You're just around the corner from the theater when you spot someone standing behind a huge bouquet of helium balloons that all say CONGRATULATIONS! Perfect. You can buy one for each of your friends. Lizette thinks that's a great idea and you head over together.

"Excuse me," you say. "How much are the balloons?"

But the balloons part and you nearly have a heart attack

when you see Shawna's smiling face looking back at you. "They're free if you can get past me!"

"*¡Que bueno!*" Lizette cries, clapping and jumping up and down. "This is great! Looks like you're the one in the hot seat now."

Gulp.

It must have been hard not letting on to Lena how disappointed you were that she didn't pick you to go with her to the birthday party. Good for you for being so understanding and realizing that fair is fair. The universe seems to be rewarding you for good behavior by giving you a crack at your own golden ticket! But are you up to the pressure cooker that the Shawna challenge can be? Stronger competitors than you have tried and failed. (Just look at poor Jasmine!) You'd better take the quiz to find out if you can keep your cool.

QUIZ TIME!

Circle your answers and tally up the points at the end.

1. You're in the middle of an oral report that you had to memorize for Spanish class and you forget the second half of your speech. What do you do?

   A. Come to a complete halt and run out of the classroom. You can barely remember how to speak English right now, let alone Spanish. True, running out mid-*examen* won't earn you any grade points with the teacher (or cool points with your friends), but it beats dealing with this pressure!

B. Struggle through it, blurting out whatever random lines of the speech you can remember. Unfortunately, you're remembering them all out of order and no one knows what you're saying. Finally you give up and beg the teacher to let you try again tomorrow.

C. Wing it. You start making things up right on the spot. You're making absolutely no sense and you're pretty sure you just said something like "Cats eat green eggs at midnight," but at least you're still talking. And maybe your teacher will be so distracted by how well you roll your *r*'s that she won't notice that your speech just went from Spanish to gibberish.

D. Stop, take a deep breath, and get your bearings. You know you can nail this speech if you just stay calm. Once you get past the nerves, the rest of the words will come flooding back to you. And if not, you'll just talk about the topic in your own words. It might not be as good as the speech, but the point is to show how well you can speak Spanish.

2. **If you could be on any game show, it would be:**

A. *Deal or No Deal.* You have plenty of time to think and ask your family and friends for help—and talk smack to the banker. And all you have to do is pick numbers, so even if you were nervous, it would still be easy to choose a case.

B. *Are You Smarter Than a 5th Grader?* The questions on this show are usually pretty easy. Plus, they give you three safety nets and you can drop out whenever you want (not that you would).

C. *Family Feud.* Coming up with answers on the spot would be a piece of cake for you. Plus, you just know you'd rock the speed round at the end.

D. *Million Dollar Password.* The whole game is a race against time. You have to give great clues or guess your partner's— all while listening to the clock tick away. Only people who are able to keep their cool do well on that show, and let's just say you'd leave with the grand prize.

3. **If you had to choose, you'd be:**

A. a yoga instructor. Half your job is teaching people how to reeelaaax. And the clothes are pretty comfy too. You don't even have to wear shoes! Talk about stress free . . .

B. a midwife. True, there is a bit of tension involved (you are helping to bring a new baby into the world, after all!) but your focus on meditation and creating a soothing atmosphere for the mom-to-be makes this a fairly mellow job.

C. a fashion-magazine editor's assistant, like Anne Hathaway in *The Devil Wears Prada.* Some girls might shy away from a job that has you running around in heels all day and night, doing a million things at once, but it looks exciting to you! Besides, when you get to enjoy some downtime, you'll be doing it in Gucci and Jimmy Choos. Totally worth the stress.

D. an ER doctor. You don't get much more high-pressure than this job. You'd get no sleep, you'd be on call twenty-four seven, and you'd have only split seconds to make life-saving decisions. The upside? You'd save a lot of people.

4. **You have a big science project due at the end of the year. You:**

A. start months and months in advance. That way you can do a little bit every day and not get overwhelmed. Why procrastinate when you could be done by Thanksgiving and not have to worry about it after that?

B. get started at least a month or so before it's due. As long as you set up a careful schedule for yourself and stick to it, you should be done just in time without breaking a sweat.

C. procrastinate until a week before it's due. You work best under pressure—or so you tell yourself. By now most of the good ideas are taken and your parents have to help you scramble for supplies, but that's all part of the fun . . . not.

D. start working on it the day it's due and end up having to beg your teacher for more time. You'll lose a letter grade and will have to sweat bullets to get it in before you fail altogether, but that date just snuck up on you!

5. **You run into your crush unexpectedly at the mall, and he says hi. You:**

A. say something that sounds like, "Uh . . . um . . . h-h-hi . . . urgh . . ." Unfortunately, your tongue always seems to tie itself into knots whenever you're around someone you like. Better just wave at him from far away next time.

B. say, "Hey," nervously, then run away like your sneakers are on fire. You're lucky you got out one word. Stay any longer and you risk serious humiliation.

C. say hi and ask him about the homework assignment from class. Maybe it's not the most stimulating conversation, but you're pretty comfortable talking about school, so it's a good way to stay calm in the face of unbelievable cuteness.

D. tell him a great joke you just heard and flirt away. Even though you weren't expecting to see him today, you immediately snap into your most practiced notice-me moves.

Give yourself 1 point for every time you answered *A*, 2 points for every *B*, 3 points for every *C*, and 4 points for every *D*.

—If you scored between 5 and 12, go to page 246.

—If you scored between 13 and 20, go to page 240.

chapter
FIFTEEN

You are one smart cookie! You'd be a shoo-in on *Jeopardy!*'s teen week, and anyone would be lucky to have you on their debate team. Some might call you a nerd, but you know that nothing is cooler than a girl with a brain. Just ask Natalie Portman, Claire Danes, Emma Watson, Michelle Obama . . .

You have arrived at what has to be one of your favorite places in the whole mall: the bookstore. What could be better than a place where you can sit and read on the floor while surrounded by stacks and stacks of books, and then go grab some hot chocolate? Gotta love that. And since you're so crazy about books, you figure Shawna might be too. Maybe she's posing as a stock girl, or she could be reading to the rug rats in the children's area. Besides, you're pretty sure the new Ann Brashares book is on sale now, and you definitely want to pick that up.

In any case, as long as you're here, you might as well start by browsing through the journals section. Some nice stationery would make the perfect bribe gift in case you do find Shawna and—*gasp*—get your question wrong. You're sifting through the different sets of stationery—would a thirteen-year-old like that lavender set with the black ribbon around it?—when you hear two people arguing behind the travel section . . . and the voices are extremely familiar. They started out whispering, but it's slowly becoming a shouting match.

"Keep it down," the guy says. "We're in a bookstore."

"Why should I?" a snotty voice answers. "Everyone who works here knows who I am, so it's not like they'll kick me out. The question is, do *you* know who I am? Do you have any idea how lucky you are to be my plus one?"

"How can I forget?" the guy answers. "You remind me every chance you get!"

Whoa. Sounds serious. You can't help yourself: You've gotta see who is causing a ruckus in the travel section. Could it really be who you think it is? You move closer to the aisle and shift some cookbooks out of your way. You peek through the stack and see . . . Jimmy and Mona! And they don't look happy at all, which makes you a little happy. You know that's terrible. But Mona is so not the girl for him. Anbody could see that.

Mona crosses her arms and narrows her eyes at Jimmy. "Well, somebody needs to remind you," she says. "I mean, you're cute and all, but I'm a model! I'm supposed to be at a photo shoot right now. You should be glad to be seen with me at all. So when I tell you to meet me somewhere at ten a.m., I mean ten a.m., not ten thirty-five. And not with a giant lump on your head that makes you look like Igor."

You wince a little at that. The lump was definitely your fault.

"Look, I told you what happened a hundred times already. And I said I was sorry about being late. I can't believe you're still mad."

"Well, believe it!" Mona snaps.

"Well, believe this," Jimmy says. "You can find yourself someone else to take to the party. I'm out."

Mona unfolds her arms and her jaw drops in shock. "What? You can't ditch me, because I'm ditching you, you loser!" Only she's saying it to his back, because he's already started to walk out of the travel section.

"Fine."

"Fine!"

After Jimmy leaves the bookstore, Mona stalks out too and walks in the opposite direction, her hair flying behind her.

Wow. You just witnessed a falling out that even Amy

Choi doesn't know about yet! You can't believe you just scooped the biggest gossip in the school. More important, you can't believe your luck: Jimmy is now as free as a bird. Would it be so far-fetched to think that maybe he'd hang with you sometime?

You've gotta call your friends to tell them the great—uh, ahem, you mean, awful, sad—news about Mona getting dumped. You are just about to hit Lena's speed-dial button when your Sidekick starts ringing with a Gwen Stefani ringtone. It's Lena.

"Oh my God, Lena, you're not going to believe this," you start, not even giving her a chance to say hi.

But she completely ignores you. *"I won! I won!"* she screams into your ear so loudly that you have to hold the phone away from you.

"What's that?" you say sarcastically. "I couldn't quite hear you. Speak up, would ya?"

"Sorry," Lena says, calming herself down a little. "But I just won a golden ticket!"

Sweet! This day is definitely looking up. First you find out that Jimmy is available again, and now your friend has just won the ticket that will get the two of you into the party of the year. Life is good!

Lena goes on to tell you that she found Shawna in the movie theater, scooping up popcorn. She had to answer a bunch of questions about Reese Witherspoon movies and then eat a small bucket of popcorn in one minute flat.

"It wasn't the most dignified thing I've ever done, but I did it. Can you believe it? *Woohoo!*" A crowd of kids in the background starts whooping it up as well.

"Whoa, it's loud there!" you tell her.

"Sorry, that's my cheering section. Isn't this great?"

"Definitely!" you yell before remembering that you're standing in the middle of a bookstore, which to you is the next best thing to a library. You lower your voice and say, "This is awesome. Now we can go to the party together! I have the perfect outfit to wear. You know that top I bought last week from Rampage? And I think I have a great idea for a birthday gift too. . . ." You trail off when you realize that Lena is being unnaturally quiet. "Um, hello? Still there, Lena?"

"Oh, um, yeah . . . I'm still here. It's just . . . well . . ."

"Spit it out. It's just me."

"Okay, well, I had kind of decided to take Jessie to the party. I mean, she is the one who practically forced me to watch *Legally Blonde*. If it weren't for her, I would have spent the summer watching The Discovery Channel. And I'm pretty sure I wouldn't have even come to the mall today if she hadn't dragged us here."

"Oh." Talk about bursting someone's bubble. Yours just exploded with a loud *pop!*

"You understand, right? You're not mad, are you? Please don't be mad."

"No, 'course not," you lie. "It's cool. I'll meet up with you guys in a few so we can celebrate, okay?"

Lena lets out a relieved sigh. "Good. See you in a . . . oh . . ."

"What's wrong now?"

"Urggh . . . you know all that popcorn I ate? Well, I think I'm going to be sick. In fact, I . . . urghh!"

The last thing you hear before Lena hangs up is the sound of her puking her guts out into the nearest trash can.

It's hard to decide how you feel right now. You hate that you missed your chance to become a model, but you're relieved you didn't have to share a stage with Mona. You feel bad for Jimmy for having to go through an ugly fight and losing his pass to the party, but you're thrilled that he's free to go on a date with someone else (preferably you). You're happy that Lena found Shawna, but you're bummed that you didn't. (And having to listen to Lena puke wasn't all that fun either.) The only thing that's clear right now is that as the best bud, you have to go congratulate your friends. But you have mixed feelings about that too. Not sure how you'll react to their good news? Take the quiz and figure it out.

QUIZ TIME!

Circle your answers and tally up the points at the end.

1.   Your friend comes to school with yet another brand-new Coach bag. You:

A. feel extremely annoyed. You don't have even one Coach bag, let alone a dozen. It feels like she's just rubbing it in your face.

B. are kind of jealous. Your friend always has the nicest things, while you are still rocking your older sister's hand-me-downs. You're glad for your friend but are upset that it never seems to be your turn.

C. feel a little embarrassed that you don't have bags as nice as hers. But it's always good to see your friend happy.

D. are in awe of your friend's hot sense of style. You're thrilled she got another bag! Just being seen with someone who owns one of those makes you feel glamorous. And if you're lucky, maybe she'll lend it to you!

2. **You've always been the youngest in the family, but your mom just had a baby. You:**

A. hate it. Say good-bye to all the special attention you used to get. Now it's baby, baby, baby every single day. The only time anyone seems to remember your name anymore is when your folks want you to change some poopy diapers.

B. could do without it. Nothing against babies or anything, but this business about skipping family game night just so you can take yet another home video of the baby? Lame.

C. feel like it's growing on you. You're not quite sure yet if you're going to like sharing the spotlight, but how could you help loving that tiny little face? Clearly the baby's an evil genius.

D. love it. You even offer to give up your own room so the baby can have more space. And you're always the first one to volunteer to change the dirty diapers. All a part of being a big sis.

3. **You try out for a plum spot on the soccer team, but another girl is given the star forward spot you wanted, while you're stuck warming the bench. You:**

   A. quit the team. What's the point of being here if you're going to spend all your time sitting on the sidelines? And who wants to play for a coach who can't recognize talent when he sees it?

   B. grumble on the bench to anyone who will listen. Somebody has to hear about what an injustice was done on the field. And you're sure they'll all agree with you.

   C. mope about it in silence. You don't agree with what the coach did, but what he says goes, so there's nothing you can do about it anyway. Might as well just try your best to put your feelings aside and support the team.

   D. become the loudest bench-warming cheerleader there is. You even offer to wear a goofy mascot costume. If you can't help your teammates by being on the field, you can at least boost their spirits like crazy!

4. **A boy you've been dating, Jake, has a friend who is going through a rough time at home, and she has started calling him to talk about it. You:**

A. forbid him to talk to her anymore and start monitoring his phone calls just in case. You know that his friend is dealing with something, but you don't want her spending too much time with Jake. You seriously doubt she just wants to be his friend.

B. feel bad for her, but don't exactly trust her motives, and you tell Jake so. Maybe you're putting him in an awkward position, but that's just how you feel.

C. are a little uneasy about it, but you don't want Jake to think you don't trust him. You keep your reservations to yourself but keep an eye on his friend all the same.

D. feel so sorry for her that you encourage Jake to spend more time with her. They're friends, after all. If you were in her position, you would hope that Jake would be there for you.

5. **You're a big pop star and are up for a Grammy this year. But the award goes to a newcomer who is being called the next big thing. You:**

A. are furious! How could she have won over you? Are those judges deaf? You storm out and vow to boycott all future awards shows.

B. clap and smile but are secretly fuming inside. You know for a fact that your album was way better than hers, but there's no accounting for taste.

C. are a little disappointed, but you've heard her album and it isn't half bad. There's always next year.

D. are happy just to have been nominated. You tell the

reporters she deserved it. She obviously worked hard and is super-talented.

Give yourself 1 point for every time you answered **A**, 2 points for every **B**, 3 points for every **C**, and 4 points for every **D**.
   —If you scored between 5 and 12, go to page 234.
   —If you scored between 13 and 20, go to page 224.

chapter SIXTEEN

How do you do it? You are one cool cucumber, no matter how stressful the situation. Not even a drill sergeant would be able to shake you. Because you can stay calm when the pressure is on, you're great at taking tests, you never panic when things go wrong, and you'd be awesome in an emergency. Just be careful not to put yourself in high-pressure situations on purpose. Just because you're good at overcoming stress doesn't mean it isn't affecting you.

Are you asleep right now? You must be, because your being here, on the set of an actual commercial, just can't be real. It's much more likely that you're curled up in your bed, drooling on your pillow, and all this is just one giant dream. You pinch yourself to make sure. *Ouch!* Okay, definitely not dreaming. *Oh my God!* This is all really happening! Now you finally know how those girls on *My Super Sweet 16* feel.

"Hey, hey, no damaging the merchandise," Steve says, winking at you.

You rub your arm briskly to get rid of any redness you may have just caused. "Right. Sorry." Thank goodness Janice wanted Steve to be here for the commercial shoot too. He's definitely less scary than she is and his presence puts you at ease. Not that you're afraid, really. You're too busy being excited to be nervous.

For the SmoothSkin Face Wash commercial, the crew has taken over a small section of the mall. While Steve was squaring away all your paperwork (thank God your mom said yes), he explained that SmoothSkin and Bebe LaRue have a long history of cross-promoting and cosponsoring events. When Bebe told SmoothSkin that some of her exclusively signed models would be allowed to promote their face wash if they agreed to shoot their next commercial in the downtown mall (more of that giving-back-to-her-hometown jazz), they went for it. Janice clearly isn't in love with the idea, but as a director, she always tries to give the client what he or she wants.

And for this commercial, what the people at SmoothSkin want is for you to frolic around the mall with a cute boy, happily spending time together, until you notice with horror that your face is all covered with pimples. So while the guy is buying you each a slice of pizza, you sneak away to the nearby pharmacy and buy a bottle of SmoothSkin Face Wash. When you come out of the store, you say your lines about how great the product is and then run to the bathroom to wash your face. Like magic, when you exit the bathroom, your pimples are gone and the guy is none the wiser. (That could never happen in real life, of course, but hey, we *are* talking about advertising here.)

They gave you a script to read while you're waiting for some last-minute lighting adjustments, and your lines seem pretty easy. But so far, there's been no sign of your costar.

"He'll be here soon," Steve assures you. "You'll be working with a great model today. He's a dream. You shouldn't have any problems. He's just taking a while because he has to remove all that makeup Sheila caked on him at the LaRue shoot."

You smile a plastic spokesmodel smile and say over-enthusiastically, "Tell him to try SmoothSkin Face Wash. It cleans your pores and doesn't dry out your skin!"

"Hey, save that for the commercial." Steve runs his hands through his Mohawk a little and then checks his watch and sighs.

"Hot date you're late for?" you ask.

"Don't I wish?" Steve answers. "It's my little brother, Bryan. He's still back at the Photo Hut. He's been waiting all day for me to drive him to the arcade. But everything's running behind schedule, and now that Janice wants me to stick around for the commercial, we may never get out of here!"

"Oh, that sucks," you say sympathetically. "I hope she didn't make you stay because of me."

Steve waves your words away as if you're being silly. "Please. It has nothing to do with you. That's just the life of an unpaid lackey!"

You guess not all jobs in "the industry" are glamorous. You never thought about it before, but someone has to do the grunt work. Looking around, you see a few people adjusting lights, one other making sure the boom mikes are secure, and one college-aged kid taking everybody's lunch order. Then there is another woman, dressed just like Janice, holding a stack of cue cards. There are wires and cords all over the place. Who knew that all this stuff was so complicated? For some reason, when you watched these commercials in the past, you always pictured somebody just filming it with a digital camcorder.

Instead, there's Janice, presiding over this carefully controlled chaos. Out of the corner of your eye, you can see a group of SmoothSkin reps, all in intimidating black suits, waiting to see you in action. Lucky for you, the outfit you have to wear—jeans and a peasant top—is so close to your usual clothes that you feel really comfortable. And since the whole point is to see how bad your skin is, they didn't put much makeup on you. You still have a number of angry pimples blooming all over your face.

Off to the side is Mr. Hadley, the pharmacy owner, and he's beaming. (Steve told you earlier that the face wash company had paid him an arm and a leg to let them use his store for the day.) Behind the barricade the crew set up, you can see a group of kids from school starting to form, all of them jostling to see what's happening on the other side. But Janice — aka The Director — is doing her best to ignore them. You can tell she's struggling to keep her cool in front of the SmoothSkin reps. Bad enough your cell phone went off while they were prepping the scene — Gwen Stefani had never sounded so loud! You knew that was Lena's ringtone, but to get that murderous look out of Janice's eyes, you just turned off your phone and tucked it away.

You are having the finishing touches put on your hair (they're positioning a small silk flower, just like the one on the bottle, above your ear) when you hear a velvety voice say, "Sorry I'm late, everybody. Sheila must have put that makeup on with superglue!"

You look up and smile at Elliott, quite possibly the best-looking guy you've ever seen. (Sorry, Jimmy.) "Elliott!" you shout in surprise. "You're my costar?"

"Yep," he answers, smiling a toothy grin. "Disappointed?"

"Huh? No! I mean . . . why didn't you tell me?"

He shrugs and raises one eyebrow playfully. "I wanted to surprise you." Well, it worked. You are surprised all right! First you find out you get to be in a commercial, and now it turns out you'll be sharing the screen with a major hottie. You can't help it: You reach out and pinch yourself again.

"Hey, hey, hey," Steve warns. "What did I tell you about damaging the merchandise?"

Elliott laughs sweetly. You are so busted.

"Right," you offer sheepishly. "Sorry about that."

At last Janice announces that it's time to take your places. She explains that in the first shot, Elliott will be chasing you around the mall, but you let him catch you.

So let's get this straight. You have to pretend that you and a really cute model are spending the day together, and he's so into you that he's chasing you around the mall? Gee. Life is tough. You go through a couple of takes, amazed at how natural it feels. Elliott keeps tickling you on this really sensitive spot on your neck, so all the laughing you're supposed to be faking is real. In fact, a few times Janice has to yell, "Cut!" just to stop you from giggling uncontrollably.

"Do I have to remind you where the light is again?" Janice yells. "Get it together!" Then she casts a guilty glance at the SmoothSkin reps. "Please," she adds.

Elliott turns toward you so Janice can't see him silently imitating her. Then he leans in and whispers, "Usually I don't mind pushing Janice's buttons. But not if it means she won't hire you again. I'll behave if you will."

"Me?" you protest. You can't help laughing a little, but you quickly get it under control.

After that the filming runs pretty smoothly. You shoot a few cute sequences by the water fountain, a few on one of the benches near the key-chain kiosk, and of course the overly dramatic scene in which you first notice that your face is covered in unsightly zits. It all goes so well . . . right up until it's time to film your lines. Elliott wishes you luck, then takes a seat behind the cameras.

"All right," Janice says, now sitting in a high canvas chair, as if she's a movie producer. All that's missing is the megaphone. "We'll give you a few minutes to run through your lines a couple of times and then we'll begin. Stephanie here will be holding your cue cards. Can you see them?"

"Can I see them? The letters are each the size of my head. They're kind of hard to miss."

Janice gives you a look that reminds you she has zero sense of humor.

"Ahem . . . I mean, yes, I can see them."

"Good." She stands up and walks behind the camera, giving you a second to steal a glance at Steve, who wipes imaginary sweat off his forehead with one hand and mouths, *Phew!*, which makes you giggle again.

You take a deep breath and read through the cue cards once, twice, a third time. The copy is not that hard to say or to memorize. The girls on *ANTM* always make the Cover-Girl commercials look like the hardest challenge. But you have a feeling you're about to show them how it's done.

"I think I'm ready," you announce, taking your place just inside the pharmacy door.

Another young intern rushes onto the set with a big black and white clapboard. "SmoothSkin Face Wash commercial, take one!" she shouts and snaps the thing closed. You're on!

"Ugh . . . It just figures. I'm having a great time with

Luke at the mall, but instead of looking my best, my face is a big ol' mess!" You gesture to your bumpy face. "The last thing I want is for him to catch me with bad skin. Just because I like pizza doesn't mean I want my face to look like one! That's why I use SmoothSkin Face Wash." You hold up the bottle to the camera. "It's made with extra aloe and vitamin A, which cleans pores and helps fight—"

"Hey! Watch it!" one of the kids from the hall yells out.

Janice starts massaging both of her temples, as if she has a migraine. *"Cut!"*

When you look over at the commotion, you see that your friends are the source of it. Lena and Jessie have shoved their way through the crowd at the barricade, which was, you guess, when Jessie stepped on Mark Bukowski's foot by accident. She's busy apologizing to Mark while Lena is flashing a ten-thousand-watt smile and waving around what looks like . . . Yes! It's a golden ticket. Awesome!

Less awesome are the death glares Janice is sending toward your friends and back at you. "I demand complete silence!" she barks.

Lena actually yelps a little and tucks the ticket into her bag. You flash her a quick thumbs-up and then put one finger over your lips. She gets it immediately. She closes an imaginary zipper over her mouth—and then one over Jessie's—and folds her hands in front of her. Even Mark and his friends straighten up a little.

When Janice is sure that the group of spectators has

been properly terrorized into silence, she turns back to you and says, "Let's try this again."

"SmoothSkin Face Wash commercial, take two!" *Snap!*

This time you can't help smiling. You know you're supposed to be bummed that your face looks like an oily pizza pie, but your friends just won tickets to the party of the year! It's beyond great. You wonder what they'll wear. . . . You don't get five words into the commercial before Janice yells out, "Cut!" for the second time.

"Excuse me, but would you mind not grinning like an idiot because your face is full of acne? You're supposed to look upset, remember? Amateurs!"

Steve runs up to you and pretends that your hair needs fluffing. "Okay, honey, time to focus. Pretend your friends aren't here, all right? Unless you want Janice to start breathing fire." He winks and runs off the set.

Right, yes. Time to focus. Third time's the charm.

The intern runs out again. "SmoothSkin Face Wash commercial, take three!" *Snap!*

This time you look right into the camera and talk as if you're just gabbing away to Jessie and Lena. "Ugh . . . It just figures. I'm having a great time with Luke at the mall, but instead of looking my best, my face is a big ol' mess!" You point to your bumpy face again. "The last thing I want is for him to catch me with bad skin. Just because I like pizza doesn't mean I want my face to look like one! That's why I use SmoothSkin Face Wash." Once again, you hold up the bottle. "It's made with extra aloe and vitamin A, which cleans pores and helps fight acne. And the moisturizing solution leaves my skin feeling soft and clean, never dry." You look off camera to where your Luke (aka Elliott) is supposedly buying you pizza. Then you whisper to the camera, "Thanks to SmoothSkin, my acne problem will be my little secret." Then you wink and dash into the bathroom.

From inside the ladies' room, you hear Janice yell, "Cut!" For a minute you think you must have messed up a line or something, but when you come out, the SmoothSkin reps are all nodding and smiling happily. And when you look over at Janice, she's smiling too. An actual smile! It's like a miracle.

"That was perfect!" she says. "That's a wrap for today, everybody. Steve, show the actress the release forms she and her mother have to sign and"—she looks back at you—"send her contact info for the agency. We'll definitely need her for the 'after' segment next week . . . and possibly for more commercial work in the future."

Elliott shoots you a wink and a big smile. And Steve does a quiet little nod-and-clap.

It's unbelievable! Not only did you get to star in a commercial, but it might be the first of many! And did Janice just call you the actress? Oh, this is *better* than being one of those ridiculously rich *My Super Sweet 16* kids. Well, it ranks pretty close, anyway. (Who are you kidding, right? Some of those kids get two cars and a private concert with Kanye West or Bow Wow. Of course, that's before they get *Exiled*.) The point is you're beyond happy.

An hour later, after you have changed back into your clothes and you're sitting with Jessie and Lena at the coffee shop, you are still unable to wipe the smile off your face.

"I can't believe it," Jessie says as she stirs her hot chocolate. "We're sitting here with a bona fide actress!"

"Please, please, no autographs," you say, pretending to be bothered by a gaggle of adoring fans.

Next to you Lena groans as she sits with her head down over her folded arms. "And I can't believe Amy actually videotaped me puking into a trash can. She sent it to everybody! A plague on her house!" She's right. Amy's viral video started making the rounds right after you left the commercial set together.

You and Jessie try to hold in your giggles. You know that Lena is embarrassed, but it *was* pretty funny. "Hey, look on the bright side: all that popcorn Shawna dared you to eat was totally worth it. You walked away with a golden ticket! Now you and Jessie will be front and center at the party."

"I guess," she groans. "But I'm leaving that out of my blog."

"No fair!" Jessie protests, her bangles tinkling wildly. "On Perez Hilton's blog, he always posts the whole ugly truth."

"Yeah, about other people!" Lena retorts.

"Minor detail," says Jessie, taking small bites from a giant chocolate chip cookie. She then blinks her big blue eyes at you, biting her lip guiltily. "About the party . . . I'm really sorry we can't take you too. It'll be extra lame without you."

But you wave her concern away. "Don't worry about it, really. I'm just glad we all actually had fun at the mall today. It must be a full moon or something! You should put that in your blog!"

"Actually, speaking of my blog . . . ," Lena says, pulling out her BlackBerry and slipping on her glasses. "We still haven't forgotten that we have a binding oral agreement about a certain comic-book geek named—"

"Hey!" you shout, interrupting Lena. "No names. Amy is still lurking around here somewhere, I'll bet."

"Well, you know who we mean," Jessie chimes. "And you might want to know that he had a big fight with Mona today in the bookstore. Amy wasn't around to catch it on tape, but supposedly it was pretty ugly, so he's no longer Mona's date to the party. And he spent that whole time at the diner asking a zillion questions about a certain super-model-slash-actress." Jessie nudges your elbow. "So the road to Jimmy is wide open for you!"

You silently look down at the table. Jimmy broke off his date with Mona and now he likes you? You really must have missed a lot while you were off trying to get famous.

But how are you going to break it to the girls that although you still have feelings for Jimmy, right now there's someone new on your mind—someone who is better-looking than you even thought possible and who really knows how to make you laugh? "The thing is," you begin, kind of wincing because you don't know how they'll react, "there's kind of . . . another guy."

To say Jessie's eyes got as big as flying saucers would be an understatement. "Oh my God! Spill it! Tell us everything!"

You're just about to tell them about Elliott when Lizette and Charlie enter the coffee shop. For the first time that day, Lizette looks happy. "Hey, movie star. How's it going?"

"You heard about the commercial? Wow, good news travels fast."

"Yeah, everybody's talking about it," Charlie says. "Well, that and Lena's tango with the trash can, of course."

"Argh . . . I am gonna *kill* Amy!" Lena says. "Who does she think she is? The real Gossip Girl?"

"I think so," Lizette answers. "She's even started signing her text messages with 'XOXO.' *Es loca esta chica.* Of course, Gossip Girl has the good sense to remain anonymous. You'll have your chance to confront Amy at the party. She just won a ticket too. Would you believe she had to look at a list of celebrity headlines and separate them into true and false?"

Jessie puts down her hot chocolate. "Are you kidding me? Talk about a piece of cake for her. She could have done that in her sleep. That would have been like asking me to accessorize a fall outfit."

Everyone nods in agreement.

"But what inquiring minds really want to know is, which cousin are you taking to the ball, Cinderella? Delia or Celia?" you ask.

Lizette's mouth spreads in a wide smile that goes from ear to ear. "Neither. I saw Charlie here crash and burn on Shawna's Wheel of Doom, so I decided to take him instead. As much as I would have loooved to take one of my annoying cousins, this was really the only fair thing to do."

"Cheers to that," Lena says, unable to hide her happiness at the news that Charlie will be at the party.

You all raise your cups to join her. "Cheers!"

Just then you hear a knock on the window where you're sitting. Everyone looks out to see Elliott, who is waving an envelope at you and motioning for you to come outside.

"Aaaaah!" both Jessie and Lizette scream at once.

"Isn't that the guy who was in the commercial with you? Why does he want to talk to you? No offense . . . ," Lizette says.

"None taken," you reply, trying to seem nonchalant when really you're doing backflips inside. "We're . . . friends."

"What?" Jessie shouts. "I received no such text message! Where is Amy Choi when you need her? Is he the guy you were talking about? Oh my God, he is sooo cute!"

"Shhh . . . ," you utter, hoping to silence her. "That

window is made of glass, not lead. He can hear you, you know."

You leave your friends in furious chatter as you make your way into the hall.

"Hey, Elliott," you say softly as you step closer to him, subconsciously twirling your hair. You're not sure why, but suddenly you're a little nervous—in a good way. "What are you doing here?"

If he's nervous, he doesn't show it at all. He's just smooth and confident, as if everything he does is on purpose. "Well, you left so quickly after we wrapped that I didn't get a chance to give you this." He hands you the envelope. "It couldn't wait until next week. It's just a little gift to say that you did a great job today and I can't wait to work with you again. I don't know if you'll be into it, but I thought you might."

"For me?" You smile so hard he can probably see every tooth in your mouth. "You didn't have to do that, but thank you," you gush as you rip open the thin white envelope to reveal . . . a golden ticket.

Not just any golden ticket. *The* golden ticket.

"No way!" you shout. "But how? This is to Shawna's birthday party. Do you even know her? Everybody's been scratching each other's eyes out for these! How did you get one from her?"

He shrugs one shoulder and smiles like it was no big deal. "Well, it helps that I'm her big brother."

Whoa! You didn't see that coming. You are stunned

into silence, which is not good, because it's your turn to speak. You just can't seem to make your mouth work.

Fortunately, he picks up the verbal slack. "Well, anyway, I guess I'll see you at the party. Or if not, see you next week when we film the rest of the commercial, okay?"

You just nod dumbly. And you're still nodding when he leans in and plants a soft kiss on your cheek and barely grazes your shoulder with his hand before he walks away.

When you finally break out of your trance enough to move, you look at the window to see Jessie so close that she's fogging up the glass as she mouths, *Oh. My.* God! That's when you finally allow yourself a disbelieving laugh at the strange, strange day you've had.

As much as you hate to admit it, the mall just might be the most exciting place on earth.

THE END

chapter SEVENTEEN

Nervous much? High-stress situations leave you feeling pretty frazzled, and being cool under pressure isn't exactly your strong suit. You try to avoid being put on the spot when you can, but like zits and bad-hair days, sometimes it is unavoidable. Instead of turning into your usual pile of nerves, take a deep breath! You may not realize it, but everybody gets jitters from time to time. The trick is not to let them get the best of you.

If Jessie had told you that by the end of the day you would be starring in your own commercial, you would have checked her forehead to see if she had a fever, because clearly she must be delirious. But here you are, standing in front of an army of cameras, getting ready to say your lines.

The idea is that you and a cute guy are having a good time in the mall when suddenly you notice that your face has broken out like crazy. (That shouldn't be too hard for you to act out, since, unfortunately, you're still a sweaty, nervous wreck and your face bears too close a resemblance to a greasy pizza.) So while he goes to get you both something to eat, you sneak off to the nearby pharmacy, buy a bottle of SmoothSkin, and say your lines about why the product is so great. Then you run into the bathroom to wash your face.

It all sounded really simple when you were reading the script. And you were pleasantly surprised to find out that Elliott would be the one starring as the guy. But now that the easy, nonspeaking parts have been filmed (mostly Elliott chasing you around the mall or playfully tickling your neck, or just holding your hand as you windowshop), it's time for the part where you have to speak. And suddenly it is way too warm in here — or is it just you? You have the sneaking suspicion that it's just you. You're convinced that whatever pimples you had before are now magnified about a million times. And although there are a small camera crew of six or seven people and only a few SmoothSkin reps, they each have two eyes, and they're all on you!

To make matters worse, word seems to have gotten around that they're shooting a commercial here. There's a crowd of kids from school forming behind the barricade, all jostling for position to get a better look at your acting debut. Great. You'll have an audience as you crash and burn. Maybe this wasn't such a good idea after all. In fact, maybe you should get out while you still can. You're just about to tell Steve that you're outta there when Janice stomps into your line of vision. Oh, right. You almost forgot about her. Quitting would mean telling Janice you've just wasted a huge chunk of her time, and then enduring her wrath. Yeah, that's so not gonna happen. Since you're not a glutton for punishment, you decide that your only option is to suck it up and get through the commercial as best you can. But seriously, did someone turn a big heater on or something? Because it is like a thousand degrees in here!

Suddenly Janice is standing in front of you, making you jump a little.

"So you see where the cue cards are, right?"

You look just over her shoulder and see the camera operator moving into position next to a woman dressed all in black, holding up a stack of cards. You nod stiffly.

"Good. Make sure you face the camera, as if you're talking to a friend. Stephanie will be holding up the cue cards with your lines on them. We'll give you a few minutes to read through them and then we'll get started."

You nod again, but inside you're in full-on panic mode. Where are Jessie and Lena when you need them? If they were here, Jessie would make goofy faces at you or something to get you to laugh, and Lena would quote some Shakespeare about calming down and rising to the challenge. But for now it looks like you're on your own. You read through the cue cards once, twice, a third time. . . .

The lines seem pretty easy. Maybe this won't be so bad after all.

Janice moves next to the camera and sits in a high canvas chair, as if she is a movie director. "Roll camera," she says loudly.

Then another intern runs out in front of you, holding up a black and white clapboard. "SmoothSkin Face Wash commercial, take one!" *You're on!*

You take a deep breath and give it your best shot. Too bad your best shot sounds a lot like "Uh-uh-uhhh, it j-j-just, um . . ."

"Cut!" Janice yells, then looks directly at you. "You want to try that again, without all the stuttering?"

Well, duh, that's what you were trying to do. But you just nod again and attempt to shake the nerves out of your body. *You can do this,* you tell yourself.

The intern runs out with the clapboard. "SmoothSkin Face Wash commercial, take two!" *Snap!*

"Ugh . . . ," you begin. "It just figures." Hey, so far so good! "I'm having a great time with Luke at the mall, but instead of looking my best, my mess is a big ol' face—"

"*Cut!*" Janice is starting to look a bit like that crab from *The Little Mermaid*. The SmoothSkin reps don't seem too thrilled either. They are looking at one another with grim faces and shaking their heads a lot. "The line is 'my face is a big ol' mess.' Again!"

"SmoothSkin Face Wash commercial, take three!" *Snap!*

"Ugh, it just figures. I'm having a great time with Luke at

the mall, but instead of looking my best, my face is a big ol' mess." You point to your face, which, by the way, is sweating bullets. "The last thing I want is for him to catch me with skin—"

"Cuuut!"

The crew is shifting around uncomfortably on their feet, and you can hear the kids by the barricade start to giggle. Even Steve cringed when you flubbed your line again.

"You don't want him to catch you with *bad* skin." Janice corrects you with a sigh. "I'm pretty sure he knows you *have* skin." That starts the kids from school laughing again. Bad idea. Janice whips around to face them and howls, "I demand absolute silence!" Her bark shuts up even Mark Bukowski, who's usually the biggest smart aleck in the bunch. Janice turns back toward you and starts rubbing her temples as if you are causing her the worst migraine headache in history. "Let's start again."

Once more the intern runs out, and you can tell she's getting tired of doing this. "SmoothSkin Face Wash commercial, take four," she says, rolling her eyes, then closing the clapboard with the loudest snap yet.

But this time you're so determined to get your lines right that you read straight through them with no emotion in your voice at all. You sound kind of like a robot. "Ugh. It. Just. Figures. I'm. Having. A. Great. Time. With. Luke. At the. Mall. And—"

"Cuuuut!"

That's pretty much how it keeps going over the next hour or so. And after you butcher take fifty-two, Janice leaps out of her canvas chair and declares, "That's it. You're fired! Steve, find me someone else . . . now!"

Steve glances at you nervously. Seeing your lip start to tremble, he gets a look of determination on his face, rushes over to Janice, and whispers something into her ear. Janice listens, raising one eyebrow. Steve gestures to the cue cards, back at you, then over to Elliott. (Yes, you've been embarrassing yourself in front of him too for the past hour.) Janice seems to weigh what Steve is saying; then she looks back in your direction and sighs. "Fine. Make the change. Everybody, take ten. I need some coffee. . . ." You've seen enough behind-the-scenes shows to know that this means "take a ten-minute break to completely freak out."

Oh no. You've totally blown this. You're not even sure what they decided to do, exactly. Maybe they're going to call the police. Can you get arrested for bad acting? If so, they're going to lock you up and throw away the key and you'll never see your friends or family again. Just as well. You've humiliated yourself in front of what seems like half the sixth-grade class. It's not like you can show your face at school, anyway.

You're waiting for your inevitable doom when you notice Steve whispering something to Elliott, who nods immediately, looks at you, and winks. He smiles and one of his chestnut curls falls over his left eye. He pushes it back with one hand and heads over to you with long, deliberate strides. "Hey," he says smoothly. "I hear you could use a hand out there."

"Just a hand?" you scoff. "What I need is an entire body transplant."

"Ah," he says, lifting your chin with his index finger. "Don't be so hard on yourself. It's not as easy as it looks, is it?"

You shrug, waves of shame radiating off you. "I guess not."

"Don't sweat it. Listen, I'm going to switch places with you. You'll be the one who goes off to buy us some food, and I'll be the one with the skin problem and all the lines. I have a feeling we'll be a great team."

Your relief is so great you're practically shaking. "Sooo . . . I'm not fired?"

"Not as long as I'm around," Elliott assures you. "But you are going to have to chill. Janice may sound like a shrew, but she's really a cute and fuzzy bunny."

Ha! You laugh unexpectedly at the image of Janice in a giant pink bunny suit. You know he said it just to loosen you up, and it worked. "Thanks," you tell him. "I needed that."

Before you know it, Elliott has gone through the makeup process to give him some fake zits, and you've gone through a quick patch job to cover your real ones. You assume they won't be showing any close-ups of your face now anyway. Again you film the scene in which the infamous pimples make their appearance. Only this time Elliott is the one who notices the zits and you're the one who goes to fetch the pizza. Then it's time for Elliott to say your—er, *his*—lines.

"Roll camera," Janice says, taking her place in the canvas chair.

And to your amazement, what you were utterly unable to say, Elliott recites as easily as if he were saying his own name. "Ugh . . . It just figures," he begins. "I'm having a great time with Lisa at the mall, but instead of looking my best, my face is a big ol' mess! The last thing I want is for her to catch me with bad skin. Just because I like pizza doesn't mean I want my face to look like one. That's why I use SmoothSkin Face Wash." He holds up the bottle with the little flower on it. "It's made with extra aloe and vitamin A, which cleans pores and helps fight acne. And the moisturizing solution leaves my skin feeling soft and clean, never dry."

He looks off camera right in your direction. He turns back and whispers, "Thanks to SmoothSkin, my acne problem will be my little secret." Then he winks and dashes into the bathroom.

"Cut!" Janice calls happily, obviously relieved finally to be working with a professional. "Now let's get set up for the bathroom sequence."

Oh, right. The only reason they weren't going to shoot the rest of the commercial now was your crummy skin condition. But with Elliott, that's not an issue. That's probably how Steve sold Janice on the idea. The casting switch means she doesn't have to come back to this "godforsaken" mall.

Right on cue, Janice approaches Elliott and air-kisses him on both cheeks. "You're a lifesaver," she tells him.

Elliott just smiles handsomely. "Anything for you, Janice."

She returns his smile, looking at him almost sweetly (as sweetly as her face can manage, anyway), and then glances your way. Whatever sweetness there was evaporates into thin air and her mouth forms a hard line. "As for you . . . Steve, give her the release forms to sign and make sure you return her wardrobe and accessories to our supply trunk before you send her back to the *mall*." She walks away without so much as a handshake, and certainly no air kisses. Well, you knew that was coming. But it still bites that you blew your chance at actually saying something in the commercial. And those passes to the Bebe LaRue wrap party at the museum? Yeah, you can forget about those too. You feel tears threatening to well up in your eyes.

"Aw, don't pay any mind to Janice," Elliott says, trying to comfort you. "She's always like that. Her daughter, Mona, is the same way."

"Wait, back up. Mona is her daughter?" So that *was* Mona you spotted at the Bebe LaRue shoot earlier. You thought Mona's modeling career was just another one of Amy Choi's exaggerations. Now it makes sense.

"Yeah, do you know her?"

"Unfortunately, yes. She goes to my school. She'll probably love it that I did such a lousy job today."

"Come on," Elliott says, draping one arm around your shoulders. "You weren't that bad."

You raise one skeptical eyebrow at him, like *Get real, dude. I was there, remember?*

He laughs a little. "Okay, maybe you were that bad. But it's just because you were nervous. You'll do way better next time."

The thought of going through this a second time fills you with dread. You shudder. "Thanks, but no thanks. I think my acting days are over. I was terrible."

He grins. "Well, you must not have been *that* terrible. Looks like you've got a couple of fans." You glance at where he's pointing and see Lena and Jessie pushing their way through the crowd still assembled behind the barricade. When Jessie sees you walking with Elliott's arm around your shoulders, her eyes practically pop out of her head. And Lena is waving a golden ticket! No way!

"Elliott, would you mind coming to meet my friends?" you ask.

"It would be my pleasure," he says, bowing with a flourish. The two of you make your way over to the now almost hyperventilating Jessie and the subdued but excited Lena. Thanks to Elliott's being by your side, the rest of the crowd is staring at you in a whole new light, your humiliating turn at acting completely forgotten (almost).

After you introduce Elliott to your friends, you grill Lena about the golden ticket in her hand. "How'd you score that?"

"Well, let's just say it involved Reese Witherspoon and a whole tub of popcorn."

"And an unfortunate run-in with a trash can," Jessie adds, then stage-whispers to you, "Lena hurled right after she won, and Amy sent the video of it to *every*body."

"Hey!" Lena said, bumping Jessie's arm. "We agreed to never speak of it again, remember?"

Jessie giggles and looks down. "My bad. But the video pretty much speaks for itself. Right now you're bigger than Beyoncé!"

Lena sighs and says, "'It is an honor I dream not of.'"

"Shakespeare, right?" Elliott offers, to Jessie's obvious shock.

Lena just looks pleasantly surprised, a smile spreading across her face. "That's right! See, Jessie? *Some* people still appreciate good literature."

"Yeah, but does he know what it means?"

Again, Elliott surprises everyone. "Sure, it means you'd rather not be famous for barfing in the mall and you wish people would just shut up about it, am I right?" he asks Lena.

She shrugs. "More or less." Then to Jessie she mumbles, "Big mouth."

"Hey, no need to get all bent out of shape," Jessie protests, swinging both fists to her hips, followed by the jangling of a dozen bangles. "If you just acted like it didn't bother you, nobody would even care about that dumb video. I mean, who talks about how Ashlee Simpson got busted lip-synching on *SNL* anymore? Nobody. And at least it wasn't as bad as the blowout I heard Jimmy and Mona had today. According to my sources, they totally had a screaming match in the bookstore a little while ago and their date is off. Pretty soon, everybody will be talking about that instead of you."

At the mention of Jimmy's name, it hits you that you haven't seen him since the crash. Even though you know Elliott is only being friendly, it's like once you met him, all thoughts of Jimmy just flew out of your head. You hope that doesn't mean you're a flake. But hearing the news that Jimmy just broke the date off with Mona, you figure he's probably going to need some time to get over that. And you had to kiss the passes to the wrap party at the museum good-bye, thanks to your supersized zits. So you wouldn't have had anything to offer Jimmy anyway.

Your promise to ask him to hang out with you is just one of many things that didn't go as planned today. The only impression you got to make on your longtime crush was on his skull; you never even made it onto the Bebe LaRue set, let alone into the photos; you completely missed out on the Shawna shenanigans; and to say you spazzed out on the commercial would be kind. If it weren't for how cool Elliott has been to you, you'd feel like the biggest loser in the world. But at least it can't get any worse.

221

Famous last words . . .

"Anyway," Lena continues, rolling her eyes at Jessie in exasperation, "I'm really sorry, but we only got one ticket, and since Jessie's the one who made me watch *Legally Blonde*, I figured she deserved the other pass." She gives Jessie another irritated look. "But I could always change my mind." Jessie smirks and sticks out her tongue at Lena. "You understand, right?" Lena says, turning to you. She bites her bottom lip and kind of winces.

And with that, the last bit of air in your balloon flies out with a *hissss*. For some reason, when you saw Lena with the golden ticket, you thought maybe all the nerves and the acne and the rejection you'd suffered today would have been worth it if you at least got to attend a killer birthday bash. Hearing that you'll be shut out of that as well is a little like taking a punch in your gut. But you don't have the heart to blame it on your friends. It would have been great to go with them, but it isn't their fault you decided to run off to try to be famous. You just shrug. "That's okay. I didn't really think I'd get to go to Shawna's birthday party, anyway."

"Shawna's party?" Elliott chimes in. Believe it or not, you'd almost forgotten he was standing there.

You and your friends look at him with puzzled faces. "You know Shawna?" you ask.

He laughs, pulling a wallet out of his back pocket and opening it to a flap of photos. In the first one, he and Shawna are standing in front of a giant Christmas tree, wearing cheesy matching sweaters. "I should," he said. "She's my sister."

"What?" the three of you say in unison, sounding a little like Celia and Delia.

"You heard me. And come to think of it . . ." He reaches into a different fold in his wallet, digging around. "I might have . . . Yep, here it is." And like a magician, he pulls out a golden ticket as if pulling a rabbit from a hat. "Shawna gave me a couple of these for my friends, and I forgot that I still had one left. You wouldn't want it, would you?" he says with a grin as he hands you the ticket.

Oh my God! After some of the most totally embarrassing hours of your life, you get to go to the party after all. You just can't hold back. You practically throw your arms around his neck and give him the biggest bear hug you can manage—instantly becoming the envy of all the girls in the crowd. You can only hope that Amy Choi is out there filming something good happening to you for once.

All in all, today was the best day at the mall you've ever had. Who says the downtown mall is the most boring place on earth? Not you!

THE END

chapter EIGHTEEN

Excellent! You are totally secure and never possessed by the green-eyed monster they call jealousy. When good things happen to your friends, you are genuinely happy for them. You don't waste time wishing you had what they have. Instead you appreciate what you have. (You do realize that these noble qualities make you a terrible candidate for most reality shows, right? But that's a good thing!)

Today hasn't exactly worked out the way you hoped, but at least Jessie and Lena are getting to go to the party. You foresee a lot of party-outfit buying in their future, with Jessie asking if a thirteen-year-old would wear this or that. As crazy as Jessie drove you with her obsessive shopping, you're kind of bummed that you won't be part of the excitement.

You are just maneuvering your way around the Auntie Em's stand in the middle of the hall when you run into Lizette and her two cousins. Lizette is holding a golden ticket in her hand while Delia and Celia argue over which one of them she should take.

"Of course she should take me," Delia says.

"Why you?" Celia answers.

"Look at me," Delia responds. "I'm obviously the cute one."

"We're identical twins, moron!"

"Only a little!"

"You can't be a little identical. You either are or you aren't."

"Well, I have this cute little mole right here on my chin that you don't have. See?"

Celia licks her thumb, reaches out, and wipes the mole right off Delia's face. "You drew that on, you psycho!"

"*¡Ay, cállate!* Both of you!" Lizette breaks in.

"Hey, don't tell us to shut up," they say in unison as they walk away together.

When Lizette notices you, she heaves a sigh and offers you a tired smile, flipping her long black curls over her shoulder. "Hi. You wouldn't want to adopt a pair of twins, would you?"

You shake your head. "I don't think so. I'm on my way to meet up with Lena and Jessie to congratulate them for winning a ticket to the party. Wanna come with?"

Lizette takes a quick look back at her cousins and says, "Let's go!"

As you walk along the mall with Lizette, passing 50 PERCENT OFF SALE signs and ducking the annoying perfume sprayers standing in front of Perfumania, you see Mark Bukowski and Jasmine Viera walking happily toward the exit, both smiling big cheesy grins—which is kind of surprising in Jasmine's case. You're not used to seeing her smile except when some teacher is assigning extra homework over the weekend or something.

"Hey, Lizette!" Jasmine cries excitedly. "I heard you got a ticket to Shawna's party. Guess we'll see you there!"

"You mean you guys won tickets too?" Lizette asks.

"Well, Mark did. But he's bringing me in exchange for tutoring him in science this year," Jasmine gushes. "Did you know that Shawna's brother is a model? He's going to be there too, with some of his *Teen Vogue* friends."

"Yeah, I heard that too. And supposedly there's going to be a giant chocolate fountain there. The guys oughta love that," Lizette adds.

"You know it!" Mark answers, pulling a golden ticket out of his back pocket. "Dude, all I had to do was sing the theme song from *SpongeBob SquarePants*." He clears his throat and belts out, "Oooooooh, who lives in a pineapple under the sea . . ."

You immediately plug your ears with your index fingers. "All right, cut it out before you summon all the dogs in the neighborhood." Maybe that was kind of mean, but it's hard being left out of all the fun. Especially after the kind of day you've had. It's bad enough that you wrecked your shot at becoming a model. But now you realize that anybody who is anybody will be at the party—and that won't include you. Bummer.

"Ha-ha, very funny." Mark smirks at you. "All I know is this gets me and Jasmine into Willy Wonka's place. Where's *your* ticket, huh?"

Well, you kind of deserved that. "Um, well, I never won one."

"Yeah, but Lena did, so she's going to take you, right? I mean, you guys have been BFFs since forever," Lizette says.

"Actually, she's taking Jessie," you admit.

"Oh."

All four of you stand there in silence for a minute, looking everywhere but at one another. It's obvious you're the only one in this group who'll be home playing Wii or watching *Hannah Montana* reruns instead of dancing with models and eating your weight in chocolate.

"*Awk*-ward . . . ," Jasmine says in a singsong voice.

She's right. But the more you think about it, the happier you are for Jessie and Lena. Yeah, it would have been great if you could all have gone together, but Jessie has been talking about this party ever since Shawna first posted the announcement on Facebook. And Lena did down a whole bucket of popcorn to win the ticket. Not to mention that when that model scout picked you out of the crowd, they were totally supportive and excited for you. So now there's no reason to rain on their parade. It's your turn to be excited for them.

You say as much to your friends. "In fact, I'm so happy for them, I'm going to buy them some celebration flowers right now. Coming, Lizette?"

"I'm in," she says, clearly grateful that the awkward moment has passed.

You wave your good-byes to Jasmine and Mark and head straight for the flower shop. That is one good thing about the mall: you can find anything here. And right now you and Lizette are cruising for some roses (Lena's favorites) or sunflowers (Jessie's faves).

The two of you are picking out some pink roses when you hear someone on the other side of the counter ask, "Do you need any help?"

That's weird, you think. The florist sounds awfully young. You didn't think they let kids work here. But when the cloud of baby's breath on the counter parts, you see that the florist is none other than Shawna herself!

"Congratulations!" she cries. "I have one more golden ticket left and it's yours . . . if you can win the last challenge of the day."

You can't believe your luck! Looks like you've still got a

shot at salvaging this day . . . if you can stop freaking out, that is.

Thank goodness! It was starting to feel like everybody had seen Shawna except you. And since nothing has gone quite as well as you'd hoped today, it would be really great if you could somehow win a ticket to the Willy Wonka-themed party. But you've heard that some of Shawna's tests are pretty tough. Are you up to the challenge? Start by seeing if you can handle this next quiz.

QUIZ TIME!

Circle your answers and tally up the points at the end.

1. You're in the middle of an oral report that you had to memorize for Spanish class and you forget the second half of your speech. What do you do?

   A. Come to a complete halt and run out of the classroom. You can barely remember how to speak English right now, let alone Spanish. True, running out mid-*examen* won't earn you any grade points with the teacher (or cool points with your friends), but it beats dealing with this pressure!

   B. Struggle through it, blurting out whatever random lines of the speech you can remember. Unfortunately, you're remembering them all out of order and no one knows what you're saying. Finally you give up and beg the teacher to let you try again tomorrow.

C. Wing it. You start making things up right on the spot. You're making absolutely no sense and you're pretty sure you just said something like "Cats eat green eggs at midnight," but at least you're still talking. And maybe your teacher will be so distracted by how well you roll your *r*'s that she won't notice that your speech just went from Spanish to gibberish.

D. Stop, take a deep breath, and get your bearings. You know you can nail this speech if you just stay calm. Once you get past the nerves, the rest of the words will come flooding back to you. And if not, you'll just talk about the topic in your own words. It might not be as good as the speech, but the point is to show how well you can speak Spanish.

2. **If you could be on any game show, it would be:**

A. *Deal or No Deal.* You have plenty of time to think and ask your family and friends for help—and talk smack to the banker. And all you have to do is pick numbers, so even if you were nervous, it would still be easy to pick a case.

B. *Are You Smarter Than a 5th Grader?* The questions on this show are usually pretty easy. Plus, they give you three safety nets and you can drop out whenever you want (not that you would).

C. *Family Feud.* Coming up with answers on the spot would be a piece of cake for you. Plus, you just know you'd rock the speed round at the end.

D. *Million Dollar Password.* The whole game is a race against time. You have to give great clues or guess your partner's—all while listening to the clock tick away. Only people who are able to keep their cool do well on that show, and let's just say you'd leave with the grand prize.

3. **If you had to choose, you'd be:**

   A. a yoga instructor. Half your job is teaching people how to reeelaaax. And the clothes are pretty comfy too. You don't even have to wear shoes! Talk about stress free . . .

   B. a midwife. True, there is a bit of tension involved (you are helping to bring a new baby into the world, after all!) but your focus on meditation and creating a soothing atmosphere for the mom-to-be makes this a fairly mellow job.

   C. a fashion-magazine editor's assistant, like Anne Hathaway in *The Devil Wears Prada.* Some girls might shy away from a job that has you running around in heels all day and night, doing a million things at once, but it looks exciting to you! Besides, when you get to enjoy some downtime, you'll be doing it in Gucci and Jimmy Choos. Totally worth the stress.

   D. an ER doctor. You don't get much more high-pressure than this job. You'd get no sleep, you'd be on call twenty-four seven, and you'd have only split seconds to make life-saving decisions. The upside? You'd save a lot of people.

4. **You have a big science project due at the end of the year. You:**

   A. start months and months in advance. That way you can do a little bit every day and not get overwhelmed. Why procrastinate when you could be done by Thanksgiving and not have to worry about it after that?

B. get started at least a month or so before it's due. As long as you set up a careful schedule for yourself and stick to it, you should be done just in time without breaking a sweat.

C. procrastinate until a week before it's due. You work best under pressure—or so you tell yourself. By now most of the good ideas are taken and your parents have to help you scramble for supplies, but that's all part of the fun . . . not.

D. start working on it the day it's due and end up having to beg your teacher for more time. You'll lose a letter grade and will have to sweat bullets to get it in before you fail altogether, but that date just snuck up on you!

5. **You run into your crush unexpectedly at the mall, and he says hi. You:**

A. say something that sounds like "Uh . . . um . . . h-h-hi . . . urgh . . ." Unfortunately, your tongue always seems to tie itself into knots whenever you're around someone you like. Better just wave at him from far away next time.

B. say, "Hey," nervously, then run away like your sneakers are on fire. You're lucky you got out one word. Stay any longer and you risk serious humiliation.

C. say hi and ask him about the homework assignment from class. Maybe it's not the most stimulating conversation, but you're pretty comfortable talking about school, so it's a good way to stay calm in the face of unbelievable cuteness.

D. tell him a great joke you just heard and flirt away. Even though you weren't expecting to see him today, you immediately snap into your most practiced notice-me moves.

Give yourself 1 point for every time you answered ***A***, 2 points for every ***B***, 3 points for every ***C***, and 4 points for every ***D***.

—If you scored between 5 and 12, go to page 246.
—If you scored between 13 and 20, go to page 240.

chapter
NINETEEN

Why such a hater? It's perfectly normal to envy other people when great things happen for them. But if you obsess over what everyone else has, you'll never fully appreciate what you have. And the green-eyed monster thing? Not a good look on anyone. Try focusing on all the stuff that makes your life special. You might find that once you do, you'll feel more secure and more trusting, and you'll be genuinely happy for others a lot more often.

Admit it. You love the merry-go-round at the south entrance. Ever since you were little, it has secretly been one of your favorite places in the mall. You and your friends always come here when you have something big to celebrate—like when Jessie finally got her braces off or when Lena won the middle school science fair. And all right, maybe you're getting a little old for this now (the saddles definitely used to seem a lot bigger), but you're powerless to resist the life-size white horses gliding up and down like a seesaw, the bright red and gold paint, and the bouncy carnival music blaring from the speakers. Besides, the ride is only twenty-five cents. Can't beat that!

Then why is it you look so miserable right now? Oh, that's right. Because this time, your so-called friends Lena and Jessie wanted to come here to celebrate winning tickets to a party that you are *not* going to. Oh sure, they said they wanted to celebrate your brush with modeling fame too, but who are they kidding? You already told them what a disaster that turned out to be. But Jessie just kind of shrugged it off and said, "Being asked to model by a Bebe LaRue scout is still pretty cool, no matter how it turned out."

So now here you all are, taking your ten-minute ride. But you didn't even have the umph to get up on a horse. Instead, you're sitting in the boring two-seater bench that doesn't move at all. Meanwhile, Jessie and Lena are sitting side by side on matching white horses attached to glittering golden poles, having way too much fun IYHO.

"Oh my God, this party is going to be such a good time!" Jessie gushes. "Shawna said she's going to have a DJ and everything."

"Not to mention the giant chocolate fountain," Lena adds. "And did Amy say something about iPod nanos in the goody bags?"

"I doubt that's true," you snap, hoping they'll catch your tone.

But Jessie either doesn't get it or just ignores it. "Yeah, I guess not," she says as her horse slides up toward the roof of the carousel and back down again. "It's probably more like iTunes gift cards, but still! I can't wait to see if there will be any celebrities there. Can you imagine if Justin Timberlake showed up and performed? That would be ginormous!"

"Hmmm," Lena hums skeptically. "I doubt he would do a thirteen-year-old's party. But the rest does sound pretty awesome. Hey, do you think her dad will dress up as Willy Wonka? That would be funny. Maybe he'll have a bunch of people dress as other characters from the book. Can't you just see Amy Choi as Violet and Mark Bukowski as Augustus?"

Jessie laughs. "Yeah, maybe. We should try to get all the guys who are going to dress up as Oompa-Loompas."

"Some of them already look like Oompa-Loompas," Lena jokes, which causes another round of wild giggling. You don't even attempt to join in—not that they notice.

"This, of course, calls for a shopping trip," Jessie insists. "Can you go tomorrow, Lena? I don't want to wait until the last minute to find something to wear."

Lena thinks as her horse bobs up and down. "I'll go on

one condition: no obsessing over what a twelve-year-old would wear versus what a thirteen-year-old would wear. And absolutely no further mention of that unfortunate popcorn-inspired incident. Promise?"

Jessie makes an X over her heart with her finger. "Cross my heart and hope to die," she agrees. "So how 'bout you?" she adds, finally turning your way. "Are you coming?"

You're sitting in the bench with your arms crossed, feeling your neck heat up with anger. "What for?" you bark. "It's not like I have anywhere special to go. While you guys are at the party, I'll be home watching *Hannah Montana* reruns, remember?"

Jessie and Lena shoot each other a quick look, and Jessie bites her lip. "God, we're such boneheads," she says. "I'm sorry. I guess I kind of forgot you aren't going to the party."

"Yeah, sorry about that," Lena adds guiltily. "But at least you aren't the only one. Even Celia and Delia got shut out. Lizette got so sick of them fighting over which one of them she would take that she decided to pick neither one. Instead, she's bringing Charlie."

"Wow, really?" Jessie asks. "Are the two of them an item now?"

"No!" Lena exclaims a little too strongly, as if the idea of Charlie being interested in Lizette bothers her. "She just felt bad for him, since he had put so much time and effort into plotting out a strategy and everything, only to choke on Shawna's challenge."

"Oh, you mean kind of like the way I crashed and burned at the photo shoot?"

Again your friends exchange a look, this time seeming a little puzzled.

"Hey, you know that's not what we meant," Lena says.

"Whatever." You are in full-on pout mode now.

"Okay, maybe we should just change the subject," Lena says wisely.

"Good idea," agrees Jessie. "So . . . can you believe summer vacation is already almost over? I can't stand that I already have to put away all my cute summer dresses and tank tops and buy some warm sweaters."

Lena shakes her head. "I know. I guess time really does fly when you're having fun."

"What fun was that?" you ask. "We spent most of the summer here in this boring mall. Lame . . ."

Now Jessie turns bright red and gets off her horse. "Oh, so now you're calling us lame?"

"So what if I am, huh?" you challenge.

Lena gets off her horse too and stands in front of you, holding on to a pole so she won't go flying as the carousel whirls around in circles. "What's your problem, anyway?"

"I don't have a problem," you say, standing up too. "I just hate this mall. This whole day blew big-time. I wish you guys had never dragged me here."

"Oh yeah? Well, don't worry. It won't happen again. I'll just leave now so you don't have to hang out with someone as *lame* as me!" With that, Jessie hops off the carousel, even though it's still moving.

"Well, that was really immature," Lena says calmly, following Jessie. "I think I'll leave this out of my blog too." The carousel keeps spinning, and by the time it circles around to where Lena and Jessie were, they're gone and the happy carnival music now just seems to be mocking you.

Between the merry-go-round and the whirlwind argument, you're dizzy! What just happened here?

Lena said it best: that was really immature. In your heart of hearts, you know it's not their fault that things didn't go well for you today. If you had rocked the photo shoot and become a big star, those two girls would have been your biggest fans. And if you had asked Jimmy out on a date, they would have been thrilled for you. So why can't you be happy for them? Looks like you've got some soul-searching to do.

QUIZ TIME!

You were still expecting a quiz? What are you, crazy? There's only one choice from here. Go to page 268 to apologize to your friends!

chapter
TWENTY

How do you do it? You are one cool cucumber, no matter how stressful the situation. Not even a drill sergeant would be able to shake you. Because you can stay calm when the pressure is on, you're great at taking tests, you never panic when things go wrong, and you'd be awesome in an emergency. But be careful: Just because you're good at overcoming stress doesn't mean it isn't affecting you.

Outside the back entrance of the mall, it's even brighter than you remember it being this morning. Shawna, with her hazel eyes twinkling, is standing in front of you, holding up a piece of white chalk. Just behind her a crowd of curious onlookers has gathered, most of them kids from school who already have their golden tickets—Lizette (along with Celia and Delia, who are back by her side and still bickering over which one of them she should take), Mark and some guys from the baseball team, Amy (who is filming the whole scene with her phone), Jasmine, Charlie, and of course Jessie and Lena. You wonder briefly if Jimmy is anywhere around too, but you can't let yourself get distracted now.

"Good luck!" Lena yells out, hopping from one foot to the other as if she has to use the bathroom. She bites her nails and looks around nervously. That's kind of how you feel inside—if the normally calm and collected Lena is this scared, you probably should be too—but you refuse to let it show. You're a little worried, though, that the chalk means Shawna is about to produce a chalk*board* and you're going to have to solve some fraction problems or something. Now, how do you get the common denominator again? Or will she ask you to find the final sale price of a top that's 20 percent off? Numbers start swirling around in your head.

"I have one golden ticket left. Are you ready to go for it?" Shawna asks you.

You shrug. "Ready as I'll ever be, I guess."

"All right, then," she says. "Assistants . . . please reveal her challenge."

Her friends Dionne and Hannah step forward to part the

crowd and reveal (drumroll, please) . . . a freshly drawn pattern of boxes with numbers in them. No way! Shawna is challenging you to a game of hopscotch.

You glance up at Jessie, who looks a little confused. No doubt she would have put hopscotch firmly in the Things a Twelve-Year-Old Would Like column, so now she'll have to rethink her whole list. But the only thing going through your mind is *Sweet!* True, it's been a long time since you've played, and your feet have definitely gotten bigger since then, but you're pretty sure you've still got the moves. All you have to do is be careful not to step on any of the lines, and aim your pieces well so they land inside the right square. No sweat. "Oh, it's so on!" you cry. Shawna has taken care of providing the game pieces you'll need to use: You each get a bottle cap. Yours is red, which you think is a lucky color. You toss a coin to see who goes first and Shawna wins.

Everybody from school forms a tight circle around the hopscotch board, clapping and cheering as Shawna begins by throwing her bottle cap down into the first square and hopping her way to the big 7 and 8 at the other end, then back to the 2, where she carefully balances on one leg and picks up her piece. Okay, so the girl's got skills. But she'll be no match for you. You throw your piece down and hop through the board in record time.

"Way to go!" you hear Lena yell.

The first few squares go by quickly. Then it gets a little harder when you get to 6 and have to toss your bottle cap into that square without it landing on any of the lines. But luckily, your nerves are made of steel. Even though your heart is beating a mile a minute, your hands are tremor free. You toss the cap and everyone hushes as they watch it land just a fraction of an inch inside the line. Whoa! That was close. There are oohs and aahs from the crowd as you leap over the 6 and land safely on the other side.

"Relax, people," you call out, feeling a little cocky now. "I'm a pro."

At long last, it's time for the final square. So far, Shawna hasn't so much as batted an eyelash, smiling confidently the whole time. But now she faces the board, her eyebrows furrowed in concentration.

"Come on, Shawna! You can do it!" Hannah whoops while Dionne claps from the sidelines. After what seems like forever, Shawna tosses her bottle cap, and it seems to move in slow motion. It flies past the 4 and 5, and right past the 6, heading straight for the big 8 in the left-hand corner. It looks like it'll be a perfect landing. But at the last second, it turns. It falls on its side and slowly rolls right out of the square. The crowd gasps.

You can't believe it. Shawna made a mistake! Now all you have to do is complete the last run-through perfectly and you win.

You stand over the board, visualizing your last throw. Finally you swing your arm forward and toss the cap, trying to be gentle but not come up short. You can't bear to look, though. So you squeeze your eyes shut and cross all ten of your fingers. It isn't until you hear the crowd erupt into cheers that you know you made it. When you open your eyes, you see your small red bottle cap lying right in the middle of the square, almost as if you had just walked over and placed it there. Unbelievable! Now all that's left is to hop over there and pick up your piece. With each square, the cheering for you gets louder, until you jump off the hopscotch board with your game piece in hand. You've *won*!

In seconds, everyone is surrounding you, slapping you on the back and cheering. Jessie breaks through the pack and gives you a high five. "Awesome job!" she yells. "That was even better than Britney's comeback tour. Now we can all go to the party together!"

Shawna walks coolly over to you, offering you her hand to shake. "You were a worthy opponent," she says, "and you won fair and square. Here's your golden ticket."

You smile and take the ticket from Shawna, then wave it in the air. "Wooohoo!" This must be how Charlie felt when Mr. Wonka told him he was giving him the whole chocolate factory.

"But wait," Lena says, joining you and Jessie. "Your ticket is good for two. So who are you gonna take?"

Jessie nudges your side with her elbow and whispers in your ear. "I hear Jimmy called off the date with Mona today. You should totally ask him!"

You have to admit that that thought has occurred to you. And you know you promised to invite Jimmy out today. But you already have someone else in mind for your ticket.

"Hey, Lizette," you call, waving her over. "How 'bout I take Celia or Delia so you don't have to choose between them?"

Lizette breaks out into a huge smile. "Are you serious?"

"Sure, why not?" you say with a shrug.

"Oh my God, you're the best!" And with that, Lizette, Celia, and Delia all close in on you and give you a rib-crushing bear hug while Lena and Jessie stand by and laugh. You can't help laughing yourself. It feels good to do the right thing and have something work out for a change. You feel like your good karma has been restored. You aren't leaving the mall with a date, and you may not have gotten to be a big-time model, but who needs that when you have good friends and a ticket to the greatest bash of the year?

THE END

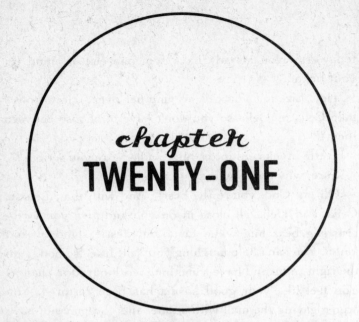

chapter
TWENTY-ONE

Nervous much? High-stress situations leave you feeling pretty frazzled, and being cool under pressure isn't exactly your strong suit. You try to avoid being put on the spot when you can, but like zits and bad-hair days, sometimes it is unavoidable. Instead of turning into your usual pile of nerves, take a deep breath! You may not realize it, but everybody gets jitters from time to time. The trick is not to let them get the best of you.

Standing just outside the back entrance of the mall, you suddenly realize how the animals at the zoo must feel. Apparently Amy found out that Shawna was about to give away her final golden ticket, and she immediately texted everybody to tell them to come outside—and come they did. She must have told the whole universe. You're not even exaggerating. You wouldn't be at all surprised if some aliens showed up. Just taking a quick glance around, you see Lizette and her two cousins; Mark and his baseball-team friends; Eli; Jasmine; Mary and Holly, the gloom-and-doom twosome (one of them holding a golden ticket); Charlie; Amy; and Jessie and Lena. You even spot Jimmy in the crowd. Suddenly you're feeling a little claustro-phobic. Everyone has formed a tight little circle around you, and they're just standing there, staring. It's as if there is some invisible force field around you and they are pow-erless to penetrate it.

Of course, the force field could have something to do with your sweating bullets. They're all keeping their dis-tance from you for the sake of their own nostrils. And is it your imagination or did the sun just get a little hotter?

"You have got to chill out," Jessie advises. "This is not good for your image. You look a little . . . nervous." That is Jessie's polite way of telling you that you're starting to look (and smell) like a wet dog. She's right, of course. You have to get it together! It's either that or make a break for it and move to Timbuktu.

But before you have a chance to contemplate how ex-actly you would get to Timbuktu, Shawna comes through the crowd, her hazel eyes sparkling in the sun.

"Thanks for waiting, everybody," she says, waving to the crowd. Then she turns to you. "If you pass this challenge, you will receive my final golden ticket. You only get one chance, and there are absolutely no do-overs. Are you ready?"

Gulp. The best you can offer are a shrug and a weak nod.

"All right. Then for the very last challenge, you will be facing . . . the Wheel of Doom!"

She pulls out a small cardboard wheel with a spinning arrow on it that you're pretty sure she got from a board game. Only now each slice of the pie has a category on it: Math, Riddles, Pop Culture, Sports, Music, or History. The crowd oohs and aahs.

"I will spin the wheel three times and wherever the arrow lands, you have to answer a question in that category. Answer all three correctly and the golden ticket is yours! Get even one of them wrong and . . ." She draws an invisible line across her neck with her index finger. "Got it?"

You nod again, looking over at your friends helplessly. What you wouldn't give to have one of them doing this instead of you. All day you knew that running into Shawna and landing in the hot seat was a possibility. You just never thought it would actually happen. But here you are and there's no backing out now. So you take a few deep breaths and try to get your heart to stop beating so loudly in your ears. A girl could go deaf listening to that!

"Here we go. . . ." Shawna spins the arrow and it whirls around the board until it finally stops on Math. Her friend Hannah steps out of the crowd, holding a box of cards. She hands one to Shawna and steps back into the circle.

"Your first question is: what is one over two plus two over four?"

"Do I get paper and a pencil?" you ask.

Shawna shakes her head. "Nope."

You take a deep breath. That problem really isn't hard. You know how to add fractions. You just have to think it through. You picture the equation in your head: $1/2 + 2/4$. All right, first things first. You have to find the common denominator. In this case it's four. And what you do to the top, you must do to the bottom, so you multiply one by two and get two over four plus two over four, and that equals four over four, which means . . .

"One!" you shout happily. "The answer is one!"

Shawna pauses the way Regis does on *Who Wants to Be a Millionaire?* "That . . . is . . . *correct*!"

Yes! Everybody starts hooting and cheering. *Thank you, Mrs. Pearl, for forcing me to learn that stuff!* you think. Who says math is useless?

Shawna quickly quiets everyone down by holding up her hands and reminding them, "She still has two questions to go!"

The crowd hushes as she sends the arrow spinning around the wheel again. This time it lands on Sports. On the sidelines you see Lena's face break into a smile. She knows that you know more about sports than some of the boys in the class.

Hannah hands Shawna another card. "Okay . . . here's

your second question: in hockey, what does it mean to pull off a hat trick?"

Easy one! "That's when a player scores three goals in one game."

Shawna pauses again, the crowd seeming to hold their breath. *"Correct!"* More cheers and whoops.

"Only one more to go, rock star!" Jessie yells. "You can do it!"

While everyone is still cheering, Shawna spins the wheel again, and this time it lands on Pop Culture. Thank goodness. You were worried you might get Riddles, and right now you're way too nervous for those. But Pop Culture? Please. You've got this in the bag.

"Hannah? The final card, please," Shawna says, holding out her hand.

Hannah steps forward and hands Shawna a white index card.

"The last question will be about *America's Next Top Model,*" Shawna informs you. Jessie and Lena give each other a high five. If there's one thing you're a certified expert on, it's that show. No way could you blow this now.

Shawna clears her throat and everyone shuts up. "This one is for all the marbles," Shawna warns. "This is your last chance. If you get this wrong, it's all over. And no one can help you. It's all on you." Jeez, no pressure or anything!

"Don't worry," you say, trying to sound confident. "I got this."

She nods her approval. "Then here's your question: who won the fourth season of the show? You've got two minutes to answer."

"Oh, that's easy. It's . . ." You trail off, drawing a complete blank. "Uh . . ." No, this can't be happening. You know this! But you just can't think. Again, you can feel the sun beating down on your head. Maybe your brain is being fried. There's no other explanation for this mental meltdown. Adults who just want to shop are trying to push past the group of kids, which has only gotten larger. And you can hear Mark taking bets on whether you're going to blow the last question. "Five dollars says she bites the dust!" he yells.

"You're on," Eli replies, digging into his pocket for the money.

"Count me in," Jasmine says, edging her way toward Charlie. Before you know it, everyone is taking one side or the other. Celia, who bet against you, is holding her throat and pretending that she's choking. Real funny.

"Come on, stop playing around!" you hear Jessie yell. "This one is easy!"

It's all just too much! And time is running out. Carrie Dee? Eva the Diva? No, neither of those is right. But you're at a total loss. You have no choice but to take a guess. "Um . . . was it . . . Jaslene?"

As soon as it comes out of your mouth, you know the answer is wrong.

"Aww . . . I'm sorry. That is incorrect. The right answer is Naima. *Nay-eee-ma*." She hands the card back to Hannah, who is waiting by her side. "Good try, though."

The jerks who bet against you are smiling happily and collecting their winnings. You glance over at your friends, and both Lena and Jessie are shaking their heads sadly.

Even Shawna looks upset for you. But then she shrugs and turns to the crowd. "Those of you who won tickets, please meet me over by the fountain so we can take a group picture."

Lena looks your way helplessly, appearing unsure of what she should do. You can tell she's been biting her nails.

"It's okay," you tell her, trying not to sound too miserable. "I could use some alone time anyway."

"Are you sure?" Jessie asks.

"Yeah, I'm fine. Go ahead."

Reluctantly, your friends head off to the fountain, where a bunch of kids with golden tickets and their guests are busily positioning themselves in what looks like a class-picture arrangement.

You don't want to rain on your friends' parade, but if you could, you would dig a hole right where you're standing and just crawl in. Since you can't do that, you slink away to a nearby bench to sulk in peace. Nothing went quite right today. You didn't end up a big-time model, it turns out your crush had a date with your worst enemy, and now you've lost out on Shawna's birthday party too. Talk about a hat trick. You probably should have just stayed in bed today.

At least it would have saved you all the humiliation you've endured. It's like you're cursed. Lucky for you it isn't possible literally to drown in self-pity, because you would definitely need a lifeguard right about now.

"Mind if I join you?" you hear someone ask.

You huff, annoyed that someone is interrupting your moping session. "Sure, if you don't mind sitting next to a loser." But when you look up, you see that the interruption is coming from your favorite artist, Jimmy Morehouse, looking as adorable as ever. If it's possible, though, he seems even mopier than you feel. The two of you could give Mary and Holly a run for their money in the gloom department. You move over on the bench immediately. "Uh, I mean, sure, have a seat."

"Thanks," he says, sitting down just inches away from you.

"So I know why I look so bummed. What happened to you?" you ask, wondering if he is feeling cursed too.

He shrugs. "Well, I had a big fight with Mona today. Looks like our date is off."

You know you shouldn't be happy about the argument, but your stomach can't help doing this pleasant little flip-flop thing, like a tiny fish is swimming around in your gut.

"Oh. Sorry to hear that," you say, wondering why he's choosing to tell you, of all people, a girl who must be exuding all kinds of loser vibes right now.

"Thanks," he says again, "but I'm all right. I think it was for the best. To be honest, I never really liked her. I just thought it might be fun to go to Shawna's party and she had a ticket. Plus, I was too shy to talk to the person I did like."

The two of you sit there quietly for a moment, neither knowing quite what to say. *So there's yet another girl waiting in the wings?* you think sadly. *Well, isn't that just the rotten cherry on top of the world's worst sundae?*

Finally he looks over at you and says, "So, what are you doing over here all by yourself? You look pretty upset for someone who just faced the Wheel of Doom and survived."

"Ha-ha," you say dryly. "As if you didn't just see me get demolished. Arggh . . ." You slap your forehead. "I still can't believe I missed such an easy question. I'm such a dope."

"Hey, hey, hey . . ." Jimmy pulls your hand down from your forehead. "I thought you did great," he says kindly. "You almost won."

You look into his sweet green eyes, realizing that the two of you are now kind of holding hands. You would be a bundle of nerves if you didn't half believe that you were just daydreaming this. "Thanks, but 'almost' didn't win me a ticket."

"True," he agrees. "But there is a silver lining there."

"Yeah?"

He looks away shyly. He takes a deep breath. "Well . . . that means we'll both be free on Saturday. So, uh, would-youwanttomaybeseeeamoviewithmeinstead?" He blurts it out so fast, you almost miss it, but there's no denying it: Jimmy just asked you to go to the movies with him. You're the other girl waiting in the wings!

Now, what should you do? Hmmm . . . decisions, decisions . . .

Just kidding! You don't need a quiz for this one. Of course you say yes!

And later that day, when you're walking home with Lena and Jessie, you will tell them in excruciating detail all about a comic-book geek and a Wheel of Doom loser, sittin' on a bench . . .

THE END

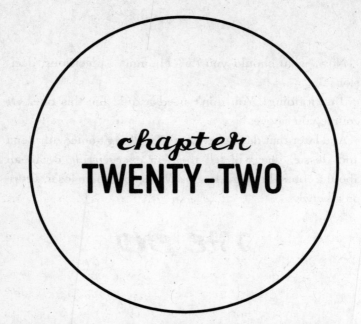

chapter TWENTY-TWO

It's great that you have such high self-esteem, but you have truly taken it to the next level! You may really be the prettiest, smartest, coolest kid in the room, but if you're conceited about it, all you'll do is drive people away. When you let others shine too, you shine that much brighter.

"I can't wait, I can't wait, I can't wait!" Jessie gushes as you and your two friends take a seat at a table in the coffee shop. "I still can't believe you won a ticket, Lena."

"Neither can I," she says, holding up the golden ticket

and inspecting it for the millionth time. "It's so pretty! This must be good-quality paper."

"Yeah," you agree, sipping your iced chai. "It's the same color gold as the Academy Award I will eventually win. You guys are so lucky you can say you knew me when."

Jessie kind of giggles. "Right. I'll have to remember to get your autograph before you start charging for it. I hear J.Lo won't sign anything if she thinks you're going to sell it on eBay."

Jessie's kidding, but you seriously believe you're on your way to the big time.

"Well, before you move to Hollywood," Lena says, "would you care to come shopping with us tomorrow? We're definitely going to need something new to wear to the party."

You grab a nearby napkin dispenser and check out your reflection. Wow, you never realized how long your neck is or how perfect your eyelashes are. Right up there with Gisele's. You sigh. "I don't know if I'll have time for stuff like that anymore," you tell Lena. "Now that I'm a model, I'm going to have real responsibilities."

Jessie and Lena exchange a look. "Is that right?" Jessie says, clearly amused.

"Well, yes. I'm going to have to start really taking care of my skin, and I'll need to get my hair done before I meet with any agents. You know how it is. Oh . . . no, I guess you don't."

Jessie's mouth drops open a little as she shoots Lena a look that says, *Can you believe this girl?* Lena just shrugs and tries to change the subject.

"Anyway . . . I was thinking I might buy that blue wrap dress we saw at Charlotte Russe," she says.

"Wow," Jessie exclaims excitedly. "Lena in a dress! You're really going to pull out all the stops!"

"I know, I know . . . ," Lena says, acknowledging her tomboy status. "But I figure an event like this calls for—"

"Do you think Tyra would want me to appear on her talk show?" you interrupt.

"What?" Lena says, unable to keep her face neutral.

"It's just, I was so good at everything today. Even Janice was impressed. And she totally knows Tyra. So maybe she would mention this young modeling prodigy she discovered today."

Jessie mouths, *Prodigy?* to Lena.

"Well, it isn't impossible," Lena says. "I guess. Although statistically, the odds would not be in your favor."

Leave it to Lena to doubt something that is clearly written in the stars.

"Anyway," Jessie continues, playing with her blond ponytail, "I'll tell you what definitely *is* possible. I think Jimmy might really like you."

You stop admiring yourself in the napkin dispenser for a minute. "Huh? But he barely talked to me today. Besides, even though I could see him ditching Mona for me, he's going on a date with her, remember?"

"Not anymore," Jessie says, leaning toward you. "Didn't you get Amy's text message? They had a big fight today and she's not taking him to the party anymore."

"Really?" you say, only half interested. "I guess I was too busy working to check some silly texts."

"Silly?" Lena repeats, crossing her arms. "We're silly now?"

You look up and see your friends frowning at you. "Oh, don't take it that way," you say. "It's just that after today, I feel like I have bigger things going on. And as for Jimmy, I'm pretty sure I can do better than him now anyway. I met this other guy, Bryan, at the shoot and he gave me his number. Besides, I mean, I'm a model! I'm going to be meeting other models and actors and stuff. Seriously, you should have seen me today at that photo shoot. Every shot was perfect. Even Mona admitted that I was way better than she expected. And you should have seen how I stood up to her! After that, everything went great. I kept working every angle, and the clothes looked so good on me, and the photographer, Jean Paul, he said that I reminded him of—"

"Oh, blah, blah, blah!" Jessie explodes. "Is this all you're going to talk about from now on?"

You lean back, shocked. Why would they want to talk about anything else? Your modeling for Bebe LaRue is huge! They said so themselves just this morning.

"I don't get it," you protest. "You guys should be happy. The modeling world loves me!"

"Oh yeah?" Lena rises from her chair and gathers her

stuff. "Then I hope you and the *modeling world*"—she drags the words out sarcastically—"will be very happy together. In the meantime, we'll just leave you alone to stare at yourself in the mirror some more, since you seem to be the only person you care about right now anyway."

"Yeah," Jessie adds. "Even J.Lo was never this much of a diva. Let us know when you have time for us little people again."

With that, they stomp out of the coffee shop, leaving you sitting there with your drink. Uh-oh. Looks like you screwed up.

Do you recognize that sound? You should. It's your own voice, which you seem to be in love with right now. Your friends get that you had a good day today and the modeling was exciting. But since when have you thought it was acceptable to be this self-absorbed? In case you didn't notice, your friends had some excitement today too, so you might want to spread around some of that enthusiasm you're lavishing on yourself.

QUIZ TIME!

No quiz this time, egomaniac! The only choice you have is clear, isn't it? You need to go apologize to your friends! Get over yourself and go to page 268.

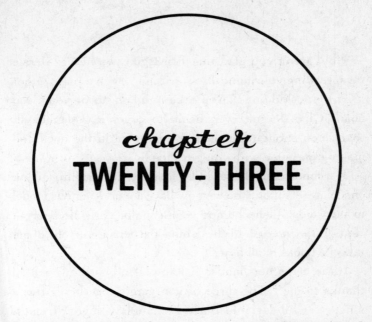

chapter
TWENTY-THREE

No one would ever accuse you of being full of yourself. You're not one to brag, even when you've got something to brag about, which is great. Just make sure you haven't eaten too big a slice of humble pie. Being proud of your achievements doesn't make you conceited—as long as you don't get a big head about it.

So remember what you were saying about the mall being the most boring place on earth? Yeah, well, scratch that. You totally take it back. Today the mall was just about the most exciting place you could even dream up.

"Now aren't you glad that I dragged you here?" Jessie says, reading your mind.

"Are you kidding?" You take another sip of your iced chai. "Glad doesn't even begin to cover it. I can never thank you enough for being a huge pain in the neck and making me come with you guys today."

"I second that," Lena adds, holding up her cup of hot chocolate. "Not only do we now have a world-famous model in our midst"—she bumps your shoulder affectionately—"but Jessie and I get to check out a party based on one of my favorite books of all time."

Jessie claps her hands. "I know! And to think, it's all thanks to me!" The three of you giggle together. After a long, stressful day, it feels good to laugh with your friends.

"I just wish we could take you too," Lena says, shooting a guilty glance your way.

"Hey, don't worry about me. I'm fine," you assure them. "Besides, I had so much fun at the photo shoot. I may not have been the best model ever, but at least I made a couple of new friends."

"Really?" Jessie says, her blue eyes popping wide open. "Who? Who? Oh, please tell me it's that gorgeous guy from the *Teen Vogue* ads. I would marry him in a heartbeat."

You drop your chin as if you're shocked. "What? I had it on good authority that your heart belongs to Robert Pattinson."

"Oh yeah . . . ," she says dreamily, sighing. "I have seen

Twilight about a million times. But hey, I have no problem with the two of them duking it out over me."

"Can we get back to the topic at hand, please?" Lena interrupts. "Who are these mystery friends of yours? One of them isn't Paris Hilton, is it? I hear she's looking for yet another BFF."

You smirk. "No, not Paris. But I might actually be able to introduce you to that *Teen Vogue* model after all." [Jessie geeks out so much at this news that it would only embarrass her to have her reaction described here. Let's just say she was happy and leave it at that.] Then you start to tell them about Steve and his brother, Bryan. But you realize you can't really describe Bryan in words—his skateboarder swagger, his sarcastic sense of humor, and his status as a hottie. So you text him, inviting him and his brother to meet you guys at the coffee shop. Hopefully he and Steve haven't left the mall yet.

"And you guys know Mona, right?" you say. "Yeah, she and I are like this now." You hold up two tightly wound fingers. "In fact, she's going to be hanging with us from now on because she thinks we're the coolest. And she's just a sweetheart."

You give yourself credit for saying all of that with a straight face.

Jessie stares at you without cracking a smile. "That's not funny. If I didn't totally need you to hobnob with the rich and famous, I'd dump this entire cup of hot chocolate over your head."

"That must have been terrible to find out you had to work with her," Jessie adds. "Was she really a total nightmare?"

You shrug and admit that yeah, at first she was. "But then we actually talked, and I think I understand her now. She just needs some real friends, I think. I feel kind of bad for her. Besides, she must not be all bad if Jimmy likes her."

"Correction: *liked* her," Lena says, holding up her phone, displaying a new text from Amy:

> Mona W. + Jimmy M. =
> Splitsville! Big scene in
> bookstore. Details TBA. XOXO

"Whoa, how did I miss that?" you exclaim, grabbing Lena's phone. "This must have just happened. Mona didn't mention anything when we were at the photo shoot. I wonder who broke off the date with who."

"Whom," Lena says, correcting you.

"Who cares?" Jessie says. "The point is their date is off, which means . . . maybe he's got another model in his heart." She winks and nudges Lena knowingly.

You wonder for a moment who they could mean. How many models could Jimmy possibly be friends with, anyway? As far as you know, the only models at school are Mona and . . . Oh!

"Who, me?" you ask, finally catching on.

"Of course you, doofus!" Jessie throws a balled-up

napkin at your head. It bounces off your cheek and lands on the table. "I've caught him looking at you once or twice at school. He might not come right out and say it, but I think he's totally into you."

"Definitely," Lena confirms.

Hmmm . . . Is it possible that Jimmy actually likes you? You have to admit you have thought about him a lot today.

But now that you've met Bryan, you aren't sure how you feel about Jimmy. Besides, if it's true that Jimmy just had a fight with Mona, he's going to need some time to get over it. When you tell your friends that, they're disappointed.

"Does that mean you're not going to invite him to the Graphic Art Museum party? Wasn't one reason you did the modeling job to get those passes so you could invite Jimmy?"

"I know, but—"

"Oh, you're just trying to weasel out of your promise to ask him to hang out with you," Jessie says accusingly. "If you don't keep your word while playing Truth or Dare, what good are you, huh?"

"I'll tell you what good I am," you say, spying Bryan and Steve walking into the coffee shop together. "What if I told you that I could get an up-and-coming designer to create some one-of-a-kind dresses for the two loveliest ladies I know to wear to Shawna's party?"

"I'd say you're my hero!" Jessie says. "Sign me up!"

Nothing like some fashion talk to effectively distract Jessie.

"But wait, is there some kind of catch?" Lena asks. "There was a catch this morning, if I recall correctly. Would this designer really be willing to make us dresses?"

"Oh, I'm sure he'd be happy to have my friends wear his designs to the most talked-about party of the year. Right, Steve?"

Steve, who is now standing right next to your table with a garment bag draped over his shoulder and a portfolio tucked under his arm, nods enthusiastically. "Uh, hellooo . . . Of course I would! That's just free advertisement for me."

After you introduce everyone and have Steve show off his killer book of designs, Jessie does a little dance in her chair. "Sweet! We are going to be the best-dressed people at the party—besides Shawna."

"Hey, don't compliment him too much. His head is already almost too big to fit through the door," Bryan says dryly.

Steve shoots him a look. "Don't pay any attention to my little brother. He's just mad because we never made it to the arcade."

But Bryan shrugs, glancing meaningfully at you. "Actually, it wasn't so bad hanging around the mall today."

You blush, smiling down at your cup of chai. You're afraid if you make eye contact with Jessie or Lena, they'll be able to tell that once again you are crushing pretty hard on someone.

But your smile is also because you're proud of yourself. You took a risk and ended up being a high-fashion model, you stood up to Mona for once, you scored passes to an exclusive Bebe LaRue party, and you made some great new friends. Not too shabby. Today was just like every other day of your life . . . except way, way better.

THE END

chapter
TWENTY-FOUR

Hate to rub this in, but the way you've been acting? Not pretty. But hopefully you realize that by now—especially since this is the last chapter of the book! Dude, otherwise you would have to go back to chapter one and try again. Luckily, you have good friends who are always willing to give you a second chance, even when you're not sure you deserve one.

"Guys, wait up!" you yell, finally spotting Jessie and Lena just as they're heading out the back entrance of the mall. It took you a while to find them, since you were in a bit of shock after they stormed away. You three have been friends a long time and you don't remember them ever being this mad at you before. Also, the mall is still full of kids from your school, some of them celebrating their golden ticket wins, so you lost sight of them in the crowd.

Thank goodness you ran into Lizette, who was walking with two very angry twins. Celia and Delia had matching scowls on their faces. And Lizette was smiling for the first time today, despite the glares being aimed in her direction.

"Hey, I heard you won a golden ticket," you said to her. "Congratulations." And as soon as you heard that word coming out of your mouth, you realized that you had never so much as congratulated your best friends in the world. All you could talk about was you, you, you. No wonder they walked out. "So which one of your cousins will you be taking?" you asked her, looking from one problem child to the other.

When Lizette just smiled but didn't say anything, Celia shouted, "Neither one of us! She's taking—"

"Some guy named Charlie," Delia continued. "I mean, can you believe that? Who chooses—"

"A guy over her own—"

"Family!" they finished in unison.

You raised an amused eyebrow at Lizette, who shook her head but didn't seem fazed at all. "Shoot! They'd been giving me the silent treatment until you came along. It was heaven. Thanks for ruining it." But you could tell from her smile that she was kidding.

"So, Charlie, huh?" you asked with a wink.

"Let me stop you right there," she urged. "It isn't like

that. Charlie is my friend, and when I saw him crash and burn on Shawna's challenge, I felt really bad for him. After all, he's spent the last week and a half plotting out every move he would make in the mall today. He deserved to win."

"So you decided to take him as your date?"

"It beats taking one of these two, who have had a rotten attitude all day and have generally driven me up the wall."

You looked at Celia and Delia and saw an uncomfortable resemblance to yourself. Was that how you'd been acting? God, you hoped not.

"Listen, have you seen Lena and Jessie?" you asked Lizette hopefully. Now that you'd seen yourself in a real mirror, you knew you had to beg your buds for forgiveness.

Once Lizette pointed you in the direction she had seen your friends going, you took off like a shot, once again putting your long legs to work. When you saw a blond ponytail bobbing along next to a brown one, moving quickly toward the door, you knew right away that those angry bobs belonged to your friends. Now here you are, begging them to give you—supermodel extraordinaire—the time of day.

"Why should we?" Jessie snaps at you.

"Look, you're right," you admit, catching up to them and running ahead so that you're standing right in their path. "I've been a little rude."

Your friends both raise one eyebrow at you, as if to say *Gimme a break. A* little *rude?*

"Okay, fine, I've been a monumental jerk."

Lena nods. "That's more like it."

"I'm really sorry," you continue. "I don't know what got into me. I guess I just got caught up in my own stuff, but I shouldn't have treated you that way. Forgive me?" You hold out your hand for one of them to shake.

Lena starts to take your hand, but Jessie reaches out and grabs her arm. "Uh-uh, not so fast. If you're really sorry, I think you should prove it."

"Prove it? But how?"

"I have an idea," Jessie says, pulling Lena a few steps away and whispering something into her ear. Lena looks your way, nods, and then whispers something back. They have the serious expressions of a couple of world leaders. You shift uncomfortably from foot to foot, wondering what they could possibly come up with that would make you feel any worse than you do right now.

Finally they walk over to you with their arms crossed and their faces grim. Lena is the first to break the silence.

"We have decided that if you want back into this friendship, you will have to answer a few trivia questions—just like Shawna would have made you answer for a ticket."

Oh good, you think. *I'm good at trivia.* Trivial Pursuit is one of your favorite games.

"But these questions will be about us," Jessie continued.

You knew there had to be a catch.

"All right. I'm ready."

"Question one," Lena announces. "What happens when a person tries to dye her own hair at home?"

You smile at the immediate memory. The three of you were in fifth grade when Jessie decided she was tired of being blond and wanted to become a redhead. Only, her mom wouldn't let her get it done. She said she was too young for that and should be happy being what she was. So the three of you saved up your money and bought an at-home dye kit, and one night when you were sleeping over at Jessie's house, you followed the instructions as best you could and dyed Jessie's hair yourselves. But you must have left it in too long, because a couple of hours later, Jessie looked less like Claire Danes in *Romeo + Juliet* and more like a giant pumpkin. Her hair was bright orange!

Jessie screamed so loudly that her mom came running. When she saw what had happened, she just shook her head—and then grounded Jessie for a week. On top of that, even though Jessie begged and begged for her mom to take her to the salon to fix her hair, her mom made her go to school like that, saying that she had to deal with the consequences of her actions. Momspeak for *See what happens when you don't listen to me?* At least Jessie was able to convince your teacher, Ms. Morgan, to let her wear a hat in class, and you and Lena wore hats too, in solidarity.

"Your hair turns a nasty shade of orange, and you and your friends end up wearing hats to school for weeks."

"Correct," Lena says, and steps back.

Jessie steps forward and clears her throat. "What are the names of Lena's four goldfish?"

You were at her house when she came home with them and let her four-year-old neighbor, Sammy, name them. "Soggy, Woggin, Drip, and Harry." You giggle a little. He was so adorable.

"All right, that was an easy one," Lena says, stepping forward. "Try this one: How long did it take each of us to run a mile in gym class?"

Again, you have to smile, because that was one of those days when you knew you had some good friends on your hands. The morning your gym teacher made the class run a mile around the track, you were getting over a cold, so you weren't in the best shape. Usually, it wouldn't have been a problem, but that day you found yourself moving turtle slow, and most of the kids in class were running circles around you. Lena was on the track team, so she probably could have run that mile in eight minutes flat, but when she saw you struggling, she slowed down and jogged beside you. Then Jessie did the same, and they both shouted their encouragement to you until the three of you crossed the finish line together and collapsed on the grass.

"It took us sixteen minutes and twelve seconds," you say proudly.

Lena smiles back at you, and Jessie, standing just behind her, shoots you a reluctant grin. You hate all that touchy-feely, mushy stuff, but when they both open their arms to you, you run in for a three-way hug. How could you even have considered tossing away their friendship? You're sure being a model would be great, but nothing beats being a regular girl with real friends.

THE END

Crystal Velasquez is the author of four books in the Maya & Miguel series: *My Twin Brother/My Twin Sister, Neighborhood Friends, The Valentine Machine,* and *Paint the Town.* She holds a bachelor's degree in creative writing from Pennsylvania State University and is a graduate of the New York University Summer Publishing Institute. Currently a production editor and freelance proofreader, she lives in Flushing, Queens, in New York City.